TO LEAVE WITH
THE REINDEER

TO LEAVE WITH THE REINDEER

THE REINDEER

Olivia Rosenthal

Translated by
Sophie Lewis

SHEFFIELD – LONDON – NEW YORK

English-language translation first published in 2019 by And Other Stories
Sheffield – London – New York
www.andotherstories.org

Copyright © Editions Gallimard, 2010

First published as *Que font les rennes après Noël?* in 2010 by Editions Verticales,
Gallimard
English-language translation © Sophie Lewis, 2019

Cover photo and inserts © 2005, Mircea Cantor, stills from the film *Deeparture*

9 8 7 6 5 4 3 2 1

This book is a work of fiction. Any resemblance to actual persons, living or
dead, events or places is entirely coincidental.

ISBN: 978-1-911508-42-7
eBook ISBN: 978-1-911508-43-4

Editor: Anna Glendenning; Copy-editor: Gesche Ipsen; Proofreader: Sarah Terry;
Typesetter: Tetragon, London; Typefaces: Linotype Swift Neue and Verlag. Printed
and bound by the CPI Group (UK) Ltd, Croydon, CR0 4YY.

A catalogue record for this book is available from the British Library.

This book is supported in part by the Institut français (Royaume-Uni) as part of
the Burgess programme (www.frenchbooknews.com), in part by English PEN's
PEN Translates programme (www.englishpen.org), supported by Arts Council
England, and in part by public funding from Arts Council England.

for Phu Si
who did not hang himself in his room

I

You don't know if you like animals but you're desperate to have one, you want a creature. This is one of the first indications of your desire, a desire that's all the fiercer for remaining unfulfilled.

Tigon, leopon, pumapard, jaglion, tiguar, jagulep, leoger, tigoness, lipard, jagress aren't only rare words, these are also creatures of flesh and blood, born in breeding centres under the observation and with the assistance of researchers dedicated to ensuring the survival of our great predators. These strange animals can't be considered truly wild for, strictly speaking, they don't exist in the natural world and belong to no recorded species. It follows that we must be legally permitted to acquire them. We have to understand nonetheless that to invite one of these specimens into our home is to put ourselves in danger, especially as scientific studies have shown that interspecies offspring frequently demonstrate severe mental problems.

You have been told that you didn't want to leave your mother's belly. There are even photos of you sitting proudly between your parent's legs, head in the air. Your breech position was the first inkling of your wilfulness.

We may wonder what 'mental problems' means for an individual resulting from the coupling of a tiger and a lioness, or a tigress and a lion, or a lioness and a leopard, or a leopard and a puma, or a jaguar and a leopardess, or of any other of the multiple combinations for which we can invent new names as required. Observers in daily contact with these creatures may have noted an abnormal tendency to docility among them, which would explain why they are classed with domestic animals and why we can, therefore, welcome them into our homes. With hybrids, everything is possible.

You've also been told that you were a magnificent baby, with a smooth head and a round, smiling face, due no doubt to your having been born by Caesarean, which spared you any physical exertion. According to family legend, your natural docility is actually born of indolence.

To find out which animal we have the right to own or tame, we must consult the laws, by-laws, statutes and decrees that differentiate the species, races and subspecies of domestic animals, the wild species, the species under threat of extinction, the wild species threatened with extinction, the protected species, species considered dangerous, and species both dangerous and protected.

You don't like wild animals. You prefer household animals, ones that live with humans as part of their families: it's those you want.

Anyone may refer to the statutory documentation to find out if they are violating the law by keeping at home a boa constrictor, a flea, a poison dart frog of the Rivan 92 cross-breed, a yellow-tailed woolly monkey, a Tibetan blue bear or a cheetah (*Acinonyx jubatus*), so charming a companion in its early years that it will jump onto your bed and lick your face before curling up at your feet. Charm is not the decisive criterion for distinguishing the wild from the domestic.

For a long time, you believed that your mother saw *Rosemary's Baby*, the Roman Polanski film, while she was pregnant with you. When, years later, you saw the film, you imagined the awful distress she must have experienced awaiting a baby that could have been human or animal.

Can we love what we don't know, can't go near, can't see, can't touch, what we imagine? Could imagination be the substrate of love?

During the very earliest years of your life, despite your docility and the perfect smoothness of your head, you showed a tendency to risk your life by rocking your cot violently or by bouts of impassioned yelling. Of this period, in which you made your presence felt with an abandon that was not to last, you have no memory.

Some wolveries, in which the trained wolves live behind bars and howl at the smallest incursion by an unfamiliar creature, may contain both wolves and 'hybrids'. The word 'hybrid', used by the trainers to reassure visitors and temper the animals' apparent ferocity, doesn't always have the intended effect.

From the age of three, you wanted a pet that would give you a break from human company. You realised that your teddy bear was not a living thing. Kissing him, yanking his ears or pulling out his fur therefore offered only moderate satisfaction.

Everyone loves teddy bears. Many people also love animals. Only, those who use them, live off them, breed them, capture them, sell them, hunt them, kill them, do not speak of love. When it comes to animals, love is a luxury that we may or may not be able to indulge. Not everyone is lucky enough to be able to love animals.

You wish you could be lucky, you wish you could be like everyone else, you wish you could say I love animals. Because when you say that, there's no need to explain, love itself is enough and exonerates us from the rest. You love animals.

From the age of three, you begged for an animal, a little ball of fur that would be entirely under your sway, in your possession, your control, in your hands, in your power: yours. Your parents refused, deciding that you wouldn't be ready to look after one, that they'd end up doing the work for you, and you felt, though you couldn't explain it, that there were deeper motivations behind this categorical refusal.

Undomesticated species are those that have not been modified by means of human selection. In contrast, domesticated species have been subject to a pressure of selection that is constant and ongoing. This pressure has resulted in the formation of a species, i.e. a group of animals which has acquired stable and genetically transmissible features, and which cannot produce fertile offspring with other species.

Rosemary's Baby tells the story of a woman who has terrible nightmares throughout her pregnancy. As she can't remember precisely the circumstances that led to her child's conception, she ends up wondering if her husband could have drugged her and allowed some vile beast to mate with her. You would like to know what effect seeing this film might have had on your mother's pregnancy.

In legal terminology, 'fertile issue' generally refers to the newborn animal, product of the coupling of two other animals, anthropomorphically known as the 'parents'. When there are no parents, this is because they have been killed or caught by predators, and likewise for humans. For a great many species, it may also occur that the animal is abandoned at birth by its so-called parents, whether because of its non-viability or excessive vulnerability, or on the contrary because it possesses innately and from the first the qualities it needs for independence and survival.

Should animals left to themselves in the wild be considered abandoned or simply independent? So long as abandonment does not become a precondition for independence.

Like many children, more even than to buy a pet you want to rescue an animal born in the wild and abandoned by its parents. Your father scolds you sharply every time you express this desire. You don't understand his anger. You keep on asking.

In France, before the passage of statute 76-629 on 10 July 1976, which introduced the concepts of environmental heritage and the conservation of species, all fauna and flora were considered *res nullius*, or belonging to no one. When something belongs to no one, anyone may take possession of it. Once a person has taken possession, this proprietor is responsible for their property, as indicated in Article 1385 of the Civil Code. 'The proprietor of an animal, or whoever makes use of an animal, is responsible during the period of its use for any damage caused by the animal, whether that animal was in his or her keeping or whether it was lost or had escaped.'

Due to this statute, of which neither your father nor your mother knows the exact terms but which they apply by intuition, you may not rescue any animal, abandoned or otherwise. Should you do that, you would become responsible for it, which, it's agreed, you're not ready for. At four years old, there is, it seems, no responsibility you may take on.

The world is a fabric of words; we are completely sheltered and sustained by the simultaneously coercive and maternal resources of the text.

You need your parents. You could die in your sleep, by choking, by putting your fingers into sockets, by spilling a bowl of hot water, by handling blunt instruments, by toppling from an open window, by falling into a pool, you are at risk, you have to be watched night and day, accidents happen so quickly, you are under the meticulous surveillance of your parents.

Wolveries are mostly established far from towns so that the wolves' howling does not disturb local people. The trainers, however, must live in close proximity to the kennels, in part to keep track of their animals' comings and goings, and in part because all training demands continual contact with the creatures one is meant to be training.

The howls you emit in the first years of your life have left no trace in your memory. Instead, you have a crystal-clear recollection of the fear you read in your mother's eyes when you used to go on all fours under the bed, or tried to hide, to escape her gaze.

There are no wild animals, there are only protected animals.

You have no experience of animals, no contact with them at all. You occasionally see them in elaborately produced films that expertly frame faces, eyes, tufts of fur, muzzles, tongues, ears, teeth, but thereby cause you to miss what's most important: the sensation and the scale of them. You miss the scale, you miss the smell, you miss the fear, you miss the sense of comparison and difference, you restrict yourself, you separate yourself, you confine yourself to those you know, you are surrounded by people who are like you. Instead of being surrounded by animals, you are surrounded by people like you.

I knew nothing about big cats, I was scraping hulls, sinking stone blocks into the seabed, I was a deepwater diver. I was spending six or seven hours at a time in the swell, I was heartily sick of it, and one day a kid I knew offered me work with some big cats. I passed a few tests the following week, I was hired, I began as a handler in a zoo, under the guidance of a trainer who showed me the ropes and, after six months, I must've had a feel for it, the boss told me this afternoon lose the overalls and take this whip, put your hand on my shoulder, now you follow me like my shadow, you're my guardian angel but you keep your trap shut, we're going into the cage together.

You love animals and you also love your mother. However, your mother does not love animals. You ask her why, why doesn't she love animals, everyone loves them, why isn't she like everyone else, you would like her, your mother, to be like everyone else, for her to look after tiny birds fallen from their nests, for her to teach them to fly, for her to rescue dogs abandoned in the woods, to feed wandering cats, to pick up hedgehogs and badgers on the roads, to bottle-feed fawns whose parents have been killed in the hunt, but your mother does not see things in the same light, she has enough to do for her own children without taking on the rest of the world's suffering, and if she did all of that, she wouldn't be your mother, the one you love more than anything in spite of her indifference to animals, she doesn't seem troubled by your demands, her confidence is such that you think she must be right: you love animals but you prefer your mother.

There's no mystery in it, to raise well-behaved animals you have to start with the babies. It depends a bit on what you want to do with them, but to make them work, you have to separate them from their mother very early and bottle-feed them yourself.

As a child, you don't speculate as to what profession you will choose, what kind of life you'll lead, where you'll live, what friends you'll have, when you'll die, what lovers you'll reject; your mother is your life, your profession, your home, your friend, your lover and everything else.

In the Justinian Code, we learn that things belonging to no one and which come under human jurisdiction may be acquired by occupancy; among these are wild animals, fish and all the other animals that live in the air, on the ground or in the sea, for natural logic has it that whatever belongs to no one may belong to whomever takes it in hand.

In the first years of your life, you think your mother owns you. Sometimes, you're sorry about this.

As I couldn't work with wolves in the beginning because you need a certificate, I started with a sheepdog. I was an alpine chasseur, I did mountain rescue. After that I got myself some Czech wolfhounds: ferocious, hard-as-nails hybrids, originally bred to guard prisoners in the Gulags and trained to attack all who try to leave the territory.

You do not attempt to leave the territory. Since learning to walk, you submit to your parents' wishes almost without complaint, you are unusually docile, unusually gentle, unusually affectionate, yet your pathological insistence that they procure the presence of a pet at your side goes on. Your parents refuse point-blank. You decide, in your own way, to defy them.

For the canine and feline species, there is a unique genealogical register in which each breed and every one of its representatives are catalogued and described. Divided into as many sections as there are breeds, this register is compiled by certified associations which define each breed's standards and which assign specimens submitted to them to one or another section according to both physical and behavioural criteria. In order to have your dog or cat join the register, you have only to prove that both of its parents are themselves registered. If this is not the case, there remains the option for your animal to take a test known as the confirmation test. During this test, the candidate is presented to the associations and examined by them. If it fulfils the criteria for belonging to a given breed, it can be 'confirmed'. This confirmation means the candidate may join the register, and its progeny too, on condition that the latter be conceived with a partner of the same breed.

You look awfully like your father, they keep on telling you. You get angry, you think that this physical resemblance shouldn't stop you, should the moment arise, from resisting him.

These are a couple of white she-wolves. They've come straight from Germany, via Belgium, that's always been the hub for buying and selling wild animals. I didn't buy them, that's illegal, I exchanged them for another pair of beasts. As I'm taming them, I spend time in the cage every day, I sit in the same place, I wear the same clothes, I make the same gestures, I wait for them to come to me and, when they're right up close, I hold my hand out to them, fist always closed so they won't attack my fingers, you never know, they're still dangerous, and I say exactly the same words so they'll get used to my voice.

You don't scream as you used to, you no longer poke your fingers into sockets, you don't turn the knobs on the oven, you don't tip over kettles and vases any more, either. You've grown used to your mother's gaze, your mother's voice, your mother's smile, to your mother's orders. But you now have the words for asking, for pro-testing, for demanding. You want an animal. You say it in your own words. You repeat them. When you feel like it, you shout them. The animals feel absent. They're so far away. They're on the other side. They're behind. They're beyond. After. Towards. Over by. Where? Where are they? Where are the animals?

If you like, we'll go into the cage together, I'll show you, follow me, don't make any sudden moves. Like this, I'm going to talk to them, hello my darlings, how are you today, come here my dears, yes my little darlings, my tabbies, my pussycats, come, come poppet, here my beauty, yes you're beautiful, hello big girl, hello my baby, what's wrong, yes of course you're beautiful, it's all OK, everything's fine, nothing's going to happen, you're my favourite little wild one, you're my sweetie-pie, you're my pussycat, everything's fine, just fine, easy now.

You're finding that the animals have gone quite far away, you're finding that they haven't come back and aren't going to come back, that you'll have to go looking for them, to hunt them and follow them into unlikely parts outside the towns, into the wastelands, overgrown meadows, fallow lands, copses, stretches of wild grass and brambles that the metropolis leaves in its wake. You decide, against your parents' wishes, that you will go in search of the animals, that you'll leave home. And to prepare for your future journey, you begin, from the age of five, to ask your parents all kinds of questions,

questions to which they give evasive replies. This confirms you in your conviction. Your parents know nothing about abandoned animals or wild children, whereas you – you will know.

Cities are not made for wolves, nor wolves for cities. When wolves appear, a crisis has occurred, upsetting cycles and regions and territories and the entire distribution of species. But we've known for decades that the distribution of species is now a human concern, and that we can redefine and redevelop territories by populating them with creatures we have chosen, exactly like a game of chess or draughts. For example, the wolves' installation in the city is now thoroughly planned out, the relevant authorities have given their consent and the logistical arrangements are on track. For a few months, the wolves will be settled, cared for, observed and fed by the two breeders who will accompany them on their journey, talk to them, reassure them, provide for them. And, assuming their stay passes without incident, we can then look ahead to establishing them in the long term, for the pleasure of old and young alike.

You don't know the Sandman, or the Bogeyman, or 'The Little Mermaid', or 'Monsieur Seguin's Goat'. Instead, thanks to a record that you've listened to over and over since you were six, you find out that children who lie to their parents may be eaten by wolves. This does not unduly frighten you. In order to lie, you would have to talk about things that happen to you, which you do as little as possible. In any case, nothing or as good as nothing does happen to you, you spend your time daydreaming your life.

It may not be immediately obvious, but rehousing wolves in a new territory demands unwavering determination. You have to fill in stacks of forms at the Ministry of the Environment and the town hall, establish contracts with feed suppliers, remember every single link in the chain, without which the slightest hiccough – a nip, a child's tumble, with the consequences we can all imagine – could take on dramatic proportions and give rise to long-running legal proceedings intended to attribute responsibility to someone, since the wolves cannot assume it. If wolves could be held responsible for the murders they commit, that would change everything. But wolves are not responsible. That responsibility, therefore, must fall to others, to a range of departments, people and offices, and will fall into the gaps and cracks in the system, should there be any. Generally, let's remember, there are no cracks.

Your father reads you very few children's stories but there's one he reads again and again, and which, for that reason, fascinates you. It's the story of Hans, a young stranger who, in order to rid a small Rhenish town of all the rats that overrun it, comes up with a strategy. He walks out by the town gates while playing a tune on his pipe, enticing the rats along behind him, enchanted and seduced by his music. The rats' eradication brings about the people's happiness.

We must not neglect the issue of housing the wolves to be kept in captivity in the city. Yes, we will house them. We will offer them trees, rocks, shelters, enclosures, dens, dwellings, holes, corners, cages, benches, polling booths, ponds, racks, cubicles, moats and public parks, and we will instal these accommodation zones in environments that are sonically, thermally, acoustically and hydrometrically adapted to their lifestyle.

The story your father tells is happy, yet it makes you uneasy. Perhaps because it's your father, usually so uncommunicative, who's telling it. Perhaps because at the end of the story he always sings a German nursery rhyme, not a word of which you understand. Perhaps because you wonder why your father speaks German. Perhaps, really, because there's a bit of the story missing.

The wolves should have access to sufficiently extensive playing fields that they can roam and run without impeding traffic and without endangering human life. To ensure this, the city plans to fit out trenches that are open to the elements yet separated from the streets by unscalably high walls. Rather than being dependent on bulldozers, pneumatic drills and mechanical diggers to build these living quarters, we'll make use of pre-existing features of the territory: abandoned archaeological digs, hydraulic barriers unused for decades due to long-term drought, former open-pit mines. While we would like the population to benefit fully from the animals' close proximity, our difficulty lies in the rarity of this kind of structure in the immediate vicinity of our cities. This is why, following due consideration, the authorities have opted to make use of castle moats. Deep, and well preserved down the centuries thanks to the high-quality materials used to build them, these are ideal for housing wolves freshly arrived from the peri-urban tundra. And they are especially suited given that in the Middle Ages, in their untouched natural settings, castles would have been surrounded by wild animals from which protection was essential. Housing wolves within our towns and in our castles will provide a timely reminder of our history.

You can't recall what becomes of Hans the piper after his adventure. Either your father always breaks off before the tale's end, or you haven't remembered the moral. Years after your father stopped reading you this kind of tale, you learn that Hans was not paid for the good turn he did the town and that upon his reappearance the inhabitants even tried to stone him in order to avoid their debt. Bent on revenge, Hans decided to use his pipe to seduce and enchant the hundred or so town children who, just like the rats, followed him out of the gates and were never seen again. In retrospect, it seems to you that, under the pretext of recapturing something of his own childhood, your father turned fairy tales to decidedly murky ends.

Introducing wolves into a city requires a degree of practical nous. The romantic dream of a return to nature is of no use to us here. Thus, we have decided against wild wolves, undomesticated wolves or those wolves, known to be dangerous, that roam freely along the border between Italy and France, crossing motorway bridges, taking tunnels and highways, slipping beneath security fences and breaking into sheepfolds by methods known only to themselves. Those wolves are not suited to a project of this scope. We will leave them to evolve in the reduced spaces of old Europe as a reminder of our archaic ancestral fears. The others, the city wolves, born in parks and fed by human hands for several generations, are easier to transplant. Moved for aesthetic, ecological, economic and touristic reasons into the aforementioned moats, they will have been selected according to strict criteria of personality and sex. We will choose members of just one family forming a single troop or pack and used to living in near-incestuous closeness. In this way, the tribe's members will be obliged to regulate the extent of their own aggression while they live together in their trenches – which by this token we will call the communal trenches.

Stories from your childhood stay on your mind for many years. You find out not only that Hans is a small-time criminal, but that *Rosemary's Baby*, the Roman Polanski film, was released in 1968, three years after your birth. Contrary to the family legend, your mother therefore could not have seen this film during her pregnancy. You wonder what use your parents meant to make of this lie, what use exactly they have made of it.

It is vital to measure in advance the degree of friendship or enmity that exists between this and that wolf in the pack and to avoid cases of flagrant hostility between brothers, cousins, parents and children. These cases are not rare. Very often, within the clan's hierarchical structure, individuals of the same sex will fight for the dominant position. Wolf is the enemy of the wolf.

You try to think of questions your parents won't be able to answer and which will force them to let you experience the world for yourself. One of these questions recurs over and over, eating at you. Where do the reindeer go after Christmas?

We have several techniques we use to set them off, you have to be patient. The best way to get them howling is to separate certain wolves from the pack, we pick one or two, separate them from the group, we handle them, they don't like it, at some point they snap, they howl to call the others, then the public really feel like they're out there on the steppe with the wild beasts, it's very impressive, genuinely awe-inspiring to hear.

When your questions become too tiresome, your parents ban you from speaking on pain of losing your tongue. You can hardly believe they'd put their threat into practice, you can't really picture them wielding sharp instruments intended to cause pain, you see them more as kindly figures and, besides, they're your parents. Despite all this you refrain, prudently, from pestering them to give you the moon. You're learning that silence can protect you.

To forestall any risk of violence within the community, we have already carefully selected the members of the troupe and begun to take the sexual drive of the females in hand by means of strategic sterilisations. These interventions must take place over the next few days. Indeed, it's best to anticipate a period of several weeks between sterilisation and the moment when the neutered animals are introduced to their new living quarters, so that those animals substantially traumatised by the scalpel have time to begin healing. The wider public must not learn that the wolves selected for them may have been mutilated before their move into the trenches. The pleasure of watching them lope around a park, encounter urban furniture and considerably modify its uses, could be wrecked by a pointless further insight into the conditions under which the whole operation has been carried out. Ecologists and animal rights campaigners often have a narrow and naïve conception of nature, and do not know that a wolf in captivity, correctly cared for and overseen by its masters, has a far greater life expectancy than that of its peers in the wild. Man is not wolf's enemy.

Your mother ventures a range of explanations for the survival of reindeer after the snow. One consists of saying they retreat to remote parts of the forest to raise their children and teach them how to pull Father Christmas's sleigh when their turn comes. You aren't sure this explanation is good enough. Even while continuing to enjoy the presents brought by their labour, you so wish they could abandon the sleigh once and for all, quit their yoke and travel as far as the farthest tundras of the East.

We are never truly friends with the animals we train. We have to keep our eyes peeled but when we enter a cage the fear vanishes, we're in our own world, we're on a totally different planet.

You imagine the reindeer racing through the snow, their flight towards the legendary East and their disappearance into the Siberian tundra. You wonder if Father Christmas makes it to these remote regions when he has to go looking for his animals. You picture him alone on foot, calling the name of each in turn for a good part of the summer as he tries to find them. But when Christmas comes round, you forget the reindeers' freedom and focus on the presents you're hoping for.

The quantity of food the wolves require will be calculated and fixed in advance by the handlers. Principally made up of unsold poultry and red meat packaged for the hypermarkets, this food will be bought at preferential prices thanks to a partnership with the shopping centre chosen to undertake daily deliveries of the meat, that is approximately 250 kg per week, or 2 kilos of meat per day, per animal.

In the circus where I used to work, it was very hard, I didn't have food for the animals, sometimes I'd see a donkey or two up on the hills, I'd head out with a sledge-hammer, the handler would come with me, all done on the sly, and we'd be back with the food by nightfall. It's a dark memory.

Your grandmother, your father's mother, is a serene and very discreet old lady. She has no stories to tell but she makes Polish dishes which she then tries to force-feed you, swinging between entreaties and commands to reinforce her case. For Easter every year, she buys a live carp, dunks it in the bathtub, lets it flail and exhaust itself, then seizes it with her bare hands and knocks it dead in the sink with a hammer, a capacity for violence unguessable from her old lady's physique. The blood spurts over the sink's enamel sides; the creature twists and fights to escape but your grandmother's triumph is total. There is never a survivor. All the carp die inexorably in her sink, one after another, and end their days in the form of that sweetish, insipid dish that you can't stand and that, with a mixture of repugnance and community pride, we call Jewish carp.

To stop the wolves taking live prey on the land allocated to them, wires and spikes aimed at preventing birds from settling within the zone should shortly be laid out. The spectacle of one of our canines tucking into a meal of mallards or swallows could really shock our fellow citizens and give rise to undue hostility towards the wolves.

You spend your weekends fishing for plastic ducks using a rod furnished with a hook. While keeping your focus on maximum efficiency, you consider how pleasurable it must be to fish for the great carp which swim in the very depths of the lake, to feel their weight on the line, to disengage the hook from each gaping mouth before throwing each one back in the water. You sense that this longing is worse even than your longing for a pet. You don't mention it to your mother. In order to lie, you'd have to speak.

There was a time when the law anticipated the breeding of species as prey for animals that fed exclusively on live creatures, but that law was amended by another, such that the wild individuals could at no juncture be described as engaged in torture, which, however, they *were*, back when all animals lived in the wild. We may recall that in those days, the predator would begin to devour its prey even before administering the final blow, a method understandably judged to be inhumane by the authorities responsible for human and animal well-being. This is why our veterinary services have transformed wolves, the big cats, snakes and bears, all traditionally partial to fresh meat, into carrion-eaters.

Your mother has decided that the assimilation of Jewish families into the French nation is sealed by their celebration of Christmas. She believes her progeny should not feel excluded from the festival all children talk about and so keenly anticipate. Therefore, you write regularly to the old white-bearded gentleman, of whom you demand a pet, a little ball of fur that you could stroke, feed, fuss over and kiss, that you could play and chatter with end-lessly and that you'd look after. But as Father Christmas does not seem to be listening, you decide that, as soon as the banquet has been consumed, you will leave with his reindeer, to take your revenge.

The chickens arrive frozen whole and we post them beneath the fence. Sometimes we stuff their rumps with beef mince and put medication in it, not antibiotics but vitamins, so the wolves' coats stay shiny. The wolf's well-being guarantees man's safety.

For one of your childhood Christmases, your parents plan a big party with all the grandmothers, grandfathers, uncles, great-uncles, aunts and great-aunts, cousins, second cousins, nieces and nephews, sons- and daughters-in-law who belong to the family by a range of crooks and branches that you have never pretended to understand. This substantial crowd squeezes into the dining room to await the moment of gift distribution. Since the previous evening, an enormous paper-covered cube has been waiting beneath the synthetic fir tree that your father consented to buy, waiting for you to open it in front of everyone. The excitement is at its peak and the ceremony is about to begin. Sitting on the floor, you tear off the wrapping in a frenzy to reveal a gigantic doll kitted out head to toe as a nurse. Your disappointment is so acute that it triggers an appalling crying fit, the cause of which nobody in the family, with all its branches and generations, can discover and which in large part spoils the festive mood of this huge reunion.

While the circumference of the accommodation zone is normally effected by means of an exterior enclosure intended to head off all attempt at escape and all unauthorised entrance, whether by people or animals, the facility envisaged here, a vast trench both deep and completely open to the skies, will require none of these structures and will therefore exhibit great architectural elegance and almost ethereal lightness. The security zone, a strip 1.5 m wide at its narrowest, that separates spectators from animals, will at a few points become a railing placed in such a way as to prevent spectators from leaning over and touching the animals. We know that children find wolves irresistible, and that mothers' vigilance can be compromised by their little ones' curiosity, unaware as they are of the gap between fairy tale and real life. For the wolf, a man is a man.

You wish you could like what the other little girls like, you'd like to play with dolls as they do, you're embarrassed that you don't play with dolls but you just can't make yourself do it, you ask for pets, soldiers, lorries, garages, teepees, superhero costumes, and by force of attrition your mother gives in to some of your wishes; you acquire the Indian outfit with feathers sticking up behind your head, and the Zorro cape, but the pet, the little ball of fur that you want to carry about with you, to fuss over, stroke, feed, look after, to which you'd confide your secrets, your sorrows, your disappointments and your desires, you'll never have that.

The open-air sections, strictly reserved for the wolves, will measure 100 m^2 at most for a couple and 20 m^2 for every additional wolf, which for a family of twelve gives an acceptable living space (300 m^2), though substantially smaller than the average area available to them in northern Canada or eastern Siberia. These sections must be enclosed by fences. The type of mesh, the spacing of the bars, the layout of the supporting posts and the different options for attaching all this to the ground have been subject to a number of studies, and the results suggest that Layher parts, with a galvanised wire mesh cladding 4 mm in diameter, will be the most appropriate and safest option. The mesh will be buried along its entire length and to a depth of 40 cm. Thus, the animals will have no means of escape.

You decide to plan your resistance to your parents' world, to proudly neglect Father Christmas, to farm snails in shoeboxes, to shelter abandoned animals in your bedroom and to leave with the reindeer after the New Year's Eve parties.

The rules are: never drop to the ground and always keep your back to the fence. For man, a wolf is a wolf.

You wonder if, in families whose closeness implies a powerful interdependence between members, introducing an individual of another species may feel like a betrayal. You would like to betray yours; you don't know how to go about it.

At night, my wolves will not be on display to the public, that's what I requested. They will have two separate dens, 23 m long, 3 m wide and up to 2.5 m high, which are the regulation dimensions. We have ordered wooden wall panels and sandy flooring; it's essential that my animals be able to relax and get some peace and quiet.

In the world of captivity just as anywhere else, animals need to distinguish day from night if we wish to spare them irreversible biological and psychological disturbance.

You realise that the stubbornness with which you continue to hope for a pet is viewed by those around you as an absurd caprice or, worse, a kind of disloyalty. You decide to accept, once and for all, that you are disloyal. You would like to betray, only you don't know how to go about it.

A system of video surveillance linked to headquarters at the castle reception will ensure the site's constant security. HQ will be connected via a telephone line on permanent standby provided by Lynx, an organisation highly respected for its effectiveness and its expertise in the surveillance of captive animals. In case of emergency, Lynx is obliged to call on the animals' sole owner and keeper. Ready to step in 24/7 and therefore housed close to the moats, the latter will have access to live-trapping equipment, a hypodermic tranquilliser gun, model Dist-Inject 55, as well as two lassos – equipment which they may not use except in the presence of the authorised veterinary doctor, who alone may provide the anaesthetic required for hypodermic restraint.

When we reach the hospital with an arm half-torn off, we don't immediately tell the nurses it was a wolf, otherwise they'd think we're mad. Still: given the size of the wound, the teeth marks in the flesh, twenty-three stitches later and a great chunk of flesh the poorer, it couldn't have been a dog. For the wolf, man is another wolf.

In time, you notice that none of the families your parents frequent has a pet. This reinforces your thought that one day you'll have to break away from those bringing you up, those who care for, cosset, fuss over, hold on to and possess you. You would like to betray them, you just don't know how to go about it.

The selection of trainers and handlers is absolutely crucial to the project's success. We will proceed through preliminary interviews with a hand-picked selection of candidates. To establish their psychological stability, we'll question them about their motivation, their background, we'll make them draw houses, trees and sheep, we'll ask them intimate questions about their childhoods and their sex lives. We will favour those demonstrating a sense of authority, instinct for organisation and responsibility, and those who also show a specific personal charm, able both to fend off the final efforts at resistance to officialdom and to ensure the support of the wider public.

You are embarrassed not to play with dolls, not to like dolls, to find dolls horrifying, you hate dolls, you never let your classmates know what you were given at Christmas, you hide the truth, you'd like to be more like the other little girls, you sometimes wonder if they're not pretending, if they wouldn't prefer, as you do, to dress up like Indians and ululate around the fire, you're not sure they're so different from you; nonetheless you envy them, you wish that, despite your revulsion, you could take a doll in your arms and rock it but you can't do it, you did try once, it was impossible, it's not that you're cold-hearted, you don't think you are, you're sure for example that you'd know how to look after a little animal, a warm, wriggling, living, breathing ball of fur. If you're not to get what you want, you'll leave with the reindeer after Christmas.

From now on, all these provisions form part of the programme to introduce wolves into the castles of France and Navarre. The head office of the veterinary services is responsible for a public awareness campaign aimed at defusing any negative reactions or occasional outbursts from sections of the population. Its role is that of arbiter between the local council and the different pressure groups active in the regions. It is particularly wary of shepherds, cattle farmers, hunting lobbies, committees of parents and local people, dog-grooming companies, societies for animal protection, circuses and museum conservationists, all of whom, with their various priorities, may be concerned by the presence of wild animals. With such a major project, anger, fear, jealousy, unthinking compassion and also the spirit of competition must be kept in check. For men, a man is a man.

For as long as you belong to your mother, you will not obtain what you want. You don't yet know how you'll go about it but one day you will betray her.

Every trainer begins their career by taking the newborns from their mother.

You wake before everyone else and usually go to spend the last hours of the night in your parents' bed. You are not sent back or scolded, you feel loved, you are strengthened by this love, you forget your childish wishes, you take up with your old teddy, you hesitate to abandon or torture it again, you're not yet ready to betray your family.

In order to prove their maternal competence, after five years' sustained fieldwork, the trainer must qualify for a certificate known as the competence certificate. This certificate allows them to be formally qualified as competent and to begin the adoption procedure with regard to one or several animals. To complete this procedure, a competent handler must fill in a multitude of coloured forms, have the animals they hope to own tagged, or have the tags of those animals already so marked registered on their incipient motherhood record.

You are beginning to wonder if you belong to your mother. You don't yet know how you'll go about it but you're determined to run away from her.

Tagging consists of the subcutaneous or intra-muscular implantation of a glass micro-cylinder containing a radio wave transponder that meets the ISO 11784 standard. Upon activation of a transceiver, a portable electronic two-way radio, the transponder answers by transmitting the animal's ID code, a unique, permanent and strictly individual code. The system's advantage lies in the reliability of its readings – which can, moreover, be taken remotely, thus allowing customs officers to avoid touching the animals. The implantation must be done at neck level (beside the jugular) on the left side.

You insisted, you begged, in the end your parents realised that your determination must find some outlet, they agreed to allow a living, wriggling, breathing animal into the household, but not the one you wanted.

The animal must also carry a passport, a green card and a CITES certificate (if it belongs to a species at risk of extinction and comes under the Washington Convention), certificates and cards that are issued by the regional environment agency and include details of the animal's origins, its identity, its date and place of birth, the ID codes of its biological father and mother, its date of entry into French territory if it comes from another country, the date of its acquisition by its current owner, height, weight, sex, identifying features. For man, the wolf is no longer a wolf.

Your parents' concession is not a major breakthrough, it's not a complete concession, only a partial climbdown; of the whole hierarchy of the animal world you do not receive the companion you were hoping for, yet you hadn't asked for the impossible, not for a horse or a panther, nor a zebra, nor even a wolfhound, you'd asked for something entirely ordinary but this has not been granted, you realise that if you didn't go about festooned in feathers, bows and arrows, if you weren't always ululating around the fire, if your tunic of skins could look something like a skirt, if you didn't go driving yellow plastic lorries, if you never bounced cars off the living room wall, if you hadn't ignored the magnificent doll you were given, if you hadn't left her to gather dust, if you hadn't at some point removed one of her arms and poked out her eyes, if you'd been less cruel to her, you might have had a claim on what you wanted, but you do not have that claim. If things don't look up, you will leave with the reindeer after Christmas. You will betray them.

Once the process is at an end, and the adoption concluded, the wolves' mother, by which we mean their keeper, may set up fixed or mobile animal accommodation, may own animals, transport them from circus to circus, from film shoot to film shoot, from one demonstration to another, from one show to another, from one town to another. When moving around or outside the region, the keeper will show all their charges' identity papers to the police, customs officers and border authorities. These papers guarantee that they are indeed the owner and master of their stock and may legally pursue commercial ends by displaying them to different audiences.

Having no claim upsets you, you're very angry at your parents, little by little you are distancing yourself from them, the absence of any pet allows you temporarily to cancel your belonging: for the moment, you no longer belong to your parents.

During each of their trips, the trainer must carry their own competence certificate, a special driving licence that the local council will provide for a fee and which authorises them to transport wild animals in the back section of their dispatch van. In any case, furnished with a microchip embedded for life behind one ear, each wolf can be identified everywhere; its traceability in European airspace and beyond is almost flawless.

When your parents are away, if only for a night, a chasm opens inside you, sleep won't come, fear rises, abandoned to your own devices you have no willpower, no wishes, no capacity for action, you're completely under their sway, in their power and possession, in their control, in their hands. Your betrayal makes no difference. You belong to your parents.

A certified competent handler's role is to educate their young, to manage this without upsetting or mistreating them, in short to establish their wolves in a captivity that is both delightful and decisive, knowing also that they will be making a living out of their captives.

You belong to no one, at least that's what you tell yourself, what you persuade yourself, what you think. You belong to no one. But there are many moments when doubt creeps in, when you weigh up the pleasure you can feel being possessed by someone, being in their hands, in their control, in their power, under their thumb, by someone who cares for you, fusses over you, nourishes you, advises you, leads you and guides you, in short, who loves you; you sometimes imagine love in this extreme form, as unreciprocated, unrestrained dependence, and the very thought of this love makes you tremble. But the trembling weakens your fighting spirit and your desire for independence. If you're going to betray them, you can't be trembling.

Certainly, it's hard to resign ourselves to making money out of those we love, to making them climb on stools, leap through flaming hoops, climb on top of shiny cars, lick the hands of make-up-caked actresses with morsels of meat hidden in their outfits for rewards. But living as we do in a mercantile society, in which parents may sell their children, their organs or their blood in order to meet life's basic requirements, we may assume that the market in wolves represents a lesser evil and stop fruitlessly resisting it.

Your parents have done the minimum, they've acquired the least bothersome creature they could find, one that demands minimal autonomy indeed. A yellow canary in a wrought-iron cage has appeared in your bedroom.

After cinema, we'd hoped to go into fashion shows but the main problem was that, teetering on their stilettos, the models couldn't keep them to heel: wolves pull too hard, the spotlights, the heat, the noise, the blaring music, it was making them jumpy, it wasn't working, we had to call time.

You haven't much affection for this canary, living, moving, almost-talking thing that it is, you can't catch it or hold it, you can only look at it and, from time to time, you open its cage door and let it flutter around in your room. To console yourself, you consider that your parents could have bought you a goldfish, in which case you wouldn't even have had the pleasure of giving it, for a few seconds, the feeling of freedom, except by dunking it in the bath like your grandmother's carp.

Wolves do sometimes succumb to heart attacks during demonstrations, and they can be diagnosed with incurable illnesses. In such cases, the certified handler will contact the vet who will take charge of euthanising the sick animal by means of lethal injection.

The day I copped it, I made a mistake, I dropped my guard, I barely had time to react and there she was, already hanging from my arm, but I'm not bitter about it, she was a wolf I knew well, I hand-reared her, we did all kinds of things together, I didn't want them to give her the shot, that would be too easy, it's always very tough when that's what we conclude, we have shared memories, we played together, took risks together, the animal really has to be suffering too much for us to go down that route, we watch them go, they look at us, they know perfectly well they're off to the abattoir, the way they have of saying goodbye by staring at you, you swallow the pill but it's not easy. Afterwards they use ovens, they put the whole animal in along with other dogs, other things, I haven't really looked into it properly, they don't burn the animals one at a time.

From an early age, you knew that you belonged to no one. Sometimes you are sorry.

The remains or cadavers must be clearly labelled. The vet will put the waste products out for the public knacker's service which is responsible for the collection and disposal of animal by-products that are unfit for human consumption. This disposal is carried out at a locally accredited incineration plant. To guarantee the waste's complete combustion, all such facilities are obliged to maintain the temperature of all resulting gases at a minimum of 850°C for at least two seconds.

One morning, you got up, the canary was lying motionless inside the cage. You tried to stand it upright, get it moving, you supported it with your fingers but it was neither breathing nor moving nor talking. It was the first time you held a dead body in your hands.

All this precaution, information, risk prevention and cadaver management must nonetheless not allow us to lose sight of what matters. The wolves' resettling in town is imminent. The municipality in question, a pioneer in this field, the veterinary services' departmental heads, the council, the office for regional amenities, have all given their green light. The file has just been passed by domestic security and by the insurers, who recognise that all precautions have been taken to ensure that no accident occurs on site. The request will shortly be ratified by the Ministry of the Environment, which will codify the potential coexistence, within a legal framework, of humans and wolves.

You went to school thinking about that small, motionless, yellow body between your fingers, that now-deceased living thing gained value in retrospect, you decided to give it a farewell ceremony in order to mark the trace of its existence, but when you got home your bird's corpse had disappeared.

Before, I used to parade with my animals, I had them all on leads, but since a young tiger scratched a kid during a street show they don't allow it any more. And people don't like us going around with cages, makes us look a bit like slave drivers, so we gave up doing that.

You'd have liked to throw the canary into the kitchen food bin yourself, wrapped in a white shroud. That would have let you give some weight to the shape of the small creature's life.

The parents have warned their children so they don't go jumping into the trenches, the locals have tightened security in their houses and apartments, there's been a spike in purchases of reinforced doors, CCTV and alarm systems of all kinds, the public–private partnership group that manages the castle moats has modified the reception area to permit bulk printing of tickets and the sale of related products. In short, the town is preparing to have its heart and soul settled by non-native specimens whose well-being and control we will ensure simultaneously. For man, the wolf is a man.

You're a child, we want to protect you, you are delicate, sensitive, we want to spare you strong emotions, you'll have plenty of time later on to discover the truth, to be horribly exposed to it. We don't want you to be exposed to the horrible truth. Determined to have your revenge, you vow to mount a reindeer after Christmas and go East with the herd.

Some condemn the monetisation of wild animals, others the irrevocable transformation of the castles into animal parks, still others would like to carry out in-depth studies of this project's impact on the local population. The authorities try to be reassuring. Information campaigns are in the pipeline ahead of the new occupants' arrival. Their installation in the town centre will change nothing about its long-term inhabitants' lives, should not cause any increased risk, will not disturb the balance between the different local communities, will not set people against each other, will not incite hostility or condemnation by the aforementioned associations. The traditions of hospitality are deep-rooted in this city.

We can say what we like but there was once a time when wolves and men lived together, so it would surprise me to find that wolves have copied humans, it must be that man has copied the wolves, the family, the tribe, all in tune, a pack leader, a clan leader, it's the same system. For men, man is a wolf.

No one has told you what happens to reindeer after Christmas. You have not had an explanation for what happens to animals' lifeless bodies. Between fairy tales and real life there is a gap that you can't seem to bridge. You fill with a mute and invisible rage. You decide that, if your parents continue to hide the truth from you, you will leave with the reindeer straight after Christmas. You will betray them.

You don't like pets, you prefer wild animals. Yet now that you watch so many wildlife programmes, wild animals have become ordinary for you.

I'm a farmer's son and the eldest of three children, my parents are farm employees, they couldn't have afforded to pay for all three of their sons to go to university. So as not to disadvantage my younger brothers, I decided to break off my studies, I had an uncle who worked in the zoo and, as luck would have it, I became a handler.

For your desire for a pet – a desire you can never fulfil – you substitute a comprehensive, obsessional and compulsive study of the whole planet's mammals. The *libido sciendi* replaces any other libido: the study blankets, the study compensates, the study cares for you, the study consoles, the study delays and deflects the desire for its object such that you take years to understand what exactly that object is and how you might access it. The study is an inexhaustible source of contentment and frustration.

The wildlife park at Vincennes is one of the oldest in Europe. It was built on the site of a temporary zoo created in the Bois de Vincennes for the 1931 Colonial Exhibition, at which you could marvel at native villages and exotic animals. Opened in 1934, the new zoo neglected the native animals to focus on those an urban public would never encounter in its immediate environment. Unlike Paris's Jardin des Plantes, the zoo's architects preferred to present its specimens in pits, upon rocky outcrops and on plateaux meant to imitate nature, avoiding bars and fences as much as possible. The building principles and hygiene rules underpinning these constructions demonstrate that those once-modern ideas about nature gradually became old-fashioned.

I am completely anti-zoo but feel I need to remain an insider so I can try to effect gradual, systemic change; to manage my team, define objectives, the most difficult species to deal with is still the handler.

You don't remember the first time you saw a mammal in the wild. There are so many first times that you've forgotten: the first time you saw a tree, the first time you ate a fruit, the first time you touched a human body that wasn't one of your family. You can't say when but you can say where: a zoo and, more precisely, the zoo at Vincennes. You can write that sentence in near certainty that you're not mistaken. The first time you saw a wild animal, it was an animal in captivity.

The mobile or stationary fittings for the units that present living specimens of local and foreign fauna to the public must keep the animals in good living conditions and allow for their oversight while also accommodating the health and safety of visitors and service staff.

The law provides without being unduly moved by irreconcilable demands. For example, reasonable living conditions would generally require that animals remain unobserved.

You hunt through reference books to learn about reindeer ethology, about their way of life and of reproduction, you learn that some are trapped in temperate regions where it snows rarely and only in tiny amounts. In any case, by age twelve, you no longer believe in Father Christmas.

No doorway nor any other access to the enclosure may be located on the public-facing side, and all doors must be equipped with airlock systems. If these doors are solid, they must be furnished with peepholes allowing complete visibility of the enclosure, without blind spots. Accessible to vans and cranes (for deliveries and maintenance), the outdoor areas will aid the animals' easy circulation. We must work particularly to avoid those bottlenecks likely to cause panic and stampedes and to lead to the fatal crushing of individuals.

You often feel like withdrawing to your bedroom but you don't dare lock your door for fear that someone in the family, attempting to open it, will realise you wanted to lock yourself in. Why should you want to lock yourself in? What reasons could you have to do so? You mustn't hide anything from your mother. For fear of having to answer these questions, which you are sure will be asked with a gentleness more hurtful and more insidious even than a telling-off, you never lock yourself in your bedroom. And you do your best to avoid anything that could justify your locking it. You want nothing more than to lock yourself in.

I've had only one telling-off worthy of the name, when I dared to go looking for tyres for the gorilla, because he had nothing in his cage, nothing at all. I was summoned by the boss who told me we're not a circus, the animals are not here for fun and games but to be sat in their cages, they have to be easy to see.

As in prisons, the captive animal must constantly be visible. But unlike prisons, everyone can come and see it, in fact the public is invited in. Showing animals to the public is one of the principal missions of zoos.

Now and then your father comes into your room without warning to do a little tidying. These are the only moments when you lose your cool and your usual equanimity turns to anger. Your father ends up backing out but that won't stop him from trying again another time. You remain on guard, you prepare to respond. You don't yet know how but one day you will escape.

Jeremy Bentham is best known for having invented, around the end of the eighteenth century, a prison design known as the panopticon, which allows a person in a central tower to observe all the prisoners in their cells, which are all aligned with the tower – without individual prisoners ever knowing if, at a given moment, they are or are not being observed. This internalisation of surveillance, or invisible surveillance, is at the heart of Bentham's plan. It was the same Bentham who, in the name of utilitarianism – a term he coined in 1781 to describe a moral and political doctrine according to which an action's worthiness is measured by the quantity of happiness it generates in the greatest number of people – the same Bentham, then, who, in his *Introduction to the Principles of Morals and Legislation* (1789), examined the place of animals in the classification of living creatures. If the respect we accord to living creatures is no longer a function of their reasoning but of their sensitivity, and by extension of their capacity for suffering – for it is always easier to read pain upon an average face than pleasure – it becomes critical to change our views on animals. The question is not: can animals speak? but: can animals suffer?

You give up on leaving with the reindeer after Christmas. You can't see how else your escape could happen. In the meantime, you are growing.

We can easily imagine how, given his knowledge and philosophical interests, Bentham would have enjoyed a commission to construct a utilitarian and panoptical wildlife park in his beloved city of London. Unluckily for him, none of his contemporaries thought of it.

You would like nothing more than to please your mother. You would like nothing more than to evade your mother's gaze. Your own ambivalence stops you from making decisions. You stay silent. You are growing.

The fixtures intended for the animals' housing must be adapted to the demands of biology, to the abilities and behaviour of each species. For primates (principally the old-world monkeys: the macaques and baboons), the public sides of their cages are lined with transparent outer walls. The completely enclosed but naturally lit viewing areas offer a minimum height of 2.5 m, surface areas of 10 m^2 for a pair of animals, with a further 2 m^2 for every additional individual. The ground will ideally be packed hard and fittings allowing the animals to climb and swing should be provided for the sake of the animals' well-being.

You have an inkling that for as long as you cannot lock yourself away, you will belong to your mother.

During humanity's eventful history, we may occasionally have shown our audiences not animals themselves but the ways some animals used to go about devouring humans. This would generally take place in jam-packed arenas and the audiences would consist of whole families there to see some Christian heads broken and to let their hair down.

You instate a strategic disorder in your bedroom. It's your way of resisting your father's repeated incursions. You are getting organised.

We've had two deaths by lions in our menagerie, seven years apart. Both times, it was human error, the handlers got themselves guzzled because they got cocky, they forgot to close a door properly, so when they open the trapdoor to let the lion into the cage the lion sees there's a bolt undone, pushes the door, finds itself in the passage face-to-face with its handlers and then, for all it's a captive, properly fed and cared for, it's still a wild animal.

You have a feeling that belonging to someone else would allow you to escape from your mother.

For a while the facilities were designed to discourage the animals from hiding in dark corners. In fact, there were no dark corners. The big cats' cages, unadorned cubes of bare concrete, looked out over a great windowed hall, inside which the visitors moved around, going from one window to the next to admire the black panther, the spotted jaguar or the tiger. Entertainment, the need to attract an audience, demanded permanent visibility. The main characters hadn't even the right to withdraw temporarily, to allow themselves a moment's intimacy.

You spend whole Saturdays in the zoological gardens, where a few emus, deer and other cervids are on show to an audience primarily attracted by the prospects of eating candyfloss, shooting BB guns and riding on carousels. You do as they do, go round on the merry-go-rounds, shoot BB guns and ride wooden horses, but you spend longer than the others in the hall of mirrors, where your unrecognisable body is reflected and distorted. For once you briefly stop observing your friends the animals. Anyway, you're disappointed by the reindeer, by the shape of their antlers, by their dull coats. You struggle to see the link between these stupid ruminants and the mounts on which you were intending to flee East, when you used to believe in Father Christmas.

After the two fatal accidents, we devoted a whole year to security, because it's not enough to say that the handler should have known better, all they had to do was not screw up, it was their fault. Especially as the stats show that a worker who always keeps the same routine has a one-in-a-thousand chance of making a mistake, which makes for a fatal error every three years; the risk of death is real.

There's no mirror in your bedroom that allows you to see your body's gradual alteration. To look at yourself, you have to go to the shared bathroom, where your parents might interrupt your observations at any moment. Rather than take this risk, you keep a close watch on your own desires.

We put in the automatic feedback system which made it physically impossible to open a cage and a sliding door at the same time, but this could not prevent every kind of accident. The handler must make the animals move from the internal compartment where they sleep to the outer cage. They clean the cage first and then, when it's ready, let the animals move into it so they can clean the sleeping compartment. Before going into the sleeping room, it's clearly written up in the protocol that the kid has to check they've all gone through, and only go in there if they've counted them all through, but that means they have to check the whole enclosure, so on some days, they set out to do their check, they bump into a mate, start chatting, the football match, did you see that goal, but holy fuck what a performance, well I never, time flies, have to make tracks, the handler goes off straight to the big cat house, sure that they've counted all their charges, though in fact that was yesterday, when they open the compartment door, oops, they're eyeballing a lion.

You use the loo as a refuge. It's the only place in the apartment where you can lock yourself in without having to explain why. There you observe the parts of you that can be seen without mirrors. As for the rest, you prudently decide to ignore them.

I came up with a system to spare the handlers any more nasty surprises. No one can go inside the big cats' sleeping compartments without a key, and that key now has to be picked up from a device set up in front of the big cats' outer cage. This way the handler is forced to recount the animals before going into the sleeping compartment. It's a system that we've been trialling for several months and it's giving excellent results.

You read animal books throughout your childhood. You've spent long periods staring at diagrams in which the predators sit at the top of pyramid constructions, so first of all you liked the strongest, the most powerful predators, the killers. You despised the little ones, those that, at the base of the pyramid, were almost certain to be eaten by all the others. You also consulted tables that compared the big cats' running times; personally, you rated the leopard for its speed at the point of attack, you were only sorry it couldn't keep going for longer. Over the years, you tended to admire the fiercest and fastest of the animals, or those judged to be so. Then there was a moment, you couldn't say exactly when or why, when the comparative interest you felt for predators and their prey was abruptly reversed.

For the lions, pumas and panthers, the observation area must be sufficiently extensive to allow the animal space for relaxation beyond public view. This depth is 7 m for the lion. It can be as little as 6 m for a puma or a panther. Further, the space must be sunlit and offer shelter from bad weather as well as shady areas where the animals can settle for naps, free of their visitors' gaze. It should be fitted either with basic bars with a maximum gap of 7 cm, or with a 25 x 15 cm solid-linked wire mesh or netting with links of 10 x 10 cm.

You learn that there's a great variety of social and sexual systems among animals. It isn't always the male who goes hunting, nor always the female who waits at home for his return, the young aren't always protected by their mother, the fathers aren't always indifferent, couples don't always stay together, the tribe isn't always a resource and a support, the males don't necessarily fight to mount the female, the females don't necessarily fight each other for their choice of male, the males aren't inevitably dominant, the females not inevitably dominated, danger doesn't always come from enemies, life isn't always a gift and you always have to defend yourself.

For the pumas, panthers and lions, the isolation cages, individual internal cages meant for short-term use, must be made so that the animals can stand upright, turn around and lie down inside them. The temperature in these is kept at 10°C; aeration through a grille and moderate natural light are requirements.

You will learn it, it's what you'll learn first of all, you always have to defend yourself. You are defending yourself.

Sexuality – this was one discovery you made not in person but through a film about life in the wild by Frédéric Rossif. Knowing how much you loved animals but having refused you the pet you begged for, your mother tried to make up for her refusal by taking you to the circus. You pretended that such efforts meant nothing to you – in fact, you used to hate all the drum-rolling, the suspense, the expectation you confusedly thought of as morbid: would the trapeze artist miss the bar and crash to the ground? Would the trainer be gobbled by his animals, or the bareback rider trampled by her galloping horse? All of this made you anxious and sad. To make a change from the mood of these outings, during which you sobbed almost non-stop, your mother opted for the art of cinema. She would take you to see great films adapted from Jules Verne in which half-mad scientists crossed vast deserts and defied nature by inventing improbable and highly spectacular machines. It was on one of these outings that you saw the Frédéric Rossif film, in which big mammals are caught on camera either out hunting, or while in rut. You learnt all at once that we both kill and copulate, and saw, for the first time, the gestures, the movements, the calls and the rhythms. Desire and death unfolded in Technicolor before you had a chance to analyse and decipher the dizzying and enduring effects of these images on your unconscious mind. Your mother was truly sorry. Next time you went to the circus.

Instead of the painted backdrops which, just a few years ago, had stood in for the residents' greenery and pandered mainly to their visitors' imaginations, animal well-being programmes introduced new vegetation somewhat closer to that of some of the animals' birth-places, or to that of their parents', grandparents', great-grandparents' and great-great-grandparents' birthplaces. The animals' environment looks marginally more like that of their ancestors, or like the places where they would have lived had everything stayed the same. But everything did not stay the same. Some regret it, others celebrate. Instead of the sad concrete slabs on which the felines used to break their claws trying to bury their faeces, eco-earth, made mainly of pine bark and disin-fectant micro-organisms, has been invented, a flooring that no longer contradicts the felines' instincts – felines have been digging to bury their droppings for genera-tions – and spares the handler their daily recourse to bleach for hygiene.

Applied to animals, a step backwards, reconstruction, restitution, in short, the state of nature, marks progress. The captives' well-being demands that we do not forget their past.

In the wild, animals don't have time for boredom. Survival, self-defence, hiding, finding shelter and food, all demand great watchfulness, rapid reactions, cunning, forward thinking, qualities that animals must deploy at an early age and which fill their days completely. In captivity, however, the range of available activities is drastically reduced. A bear that would usually spend eight hours a day looking for food will take ten minutes to polish off its bowlful. The rest of the time it has nothing to do, its cage is round so it goes round and round, it picks up the standard tics, it grows bored; if it is not to go into decline, we must find something for it to do.

In the absence of further trips with your mother to discover sex, violence, nature and death via the art of cinema, you watch TV series. You have a feeling that nothing ever happens to you.

For example, to prevent the monkeys eating their meals too quickly, we hide the food inside boxes, in twists of paper, in mazes, so that to reach their bananas and seeds they have to come up with all kinds of strategies, to use a range of tools that we provide for them.

You watch *Skippy*, *Daktari* and *Flipper*. These series show the adventures of wild animals tamed by men and living peacefully alongside them. Poachers and traffickers of arms, fur and wild meat are forever interfering with these paradises, trying to burn down the reserve, to ransack the safari park, to steal and resell the best-trained animals, even to kill the sanctuary guardians. Luckily, a short-sighted lion, a clever chimp, a chatty dolphin and a feisty kangaroo are ready to ensure the renewed delight of those children who, on Thursday afternoons when there's no school, are allowed exceptionally to turn on the small screen and break up the long march of those empty hours. Were paradise not endangered, you'd not even know how to kill time trying to save it. More than on all the other days, on Thursday afternoons you are bored. Boredom is worse than anything, it's worse than death.

In the wild, well-being coincides with an ephemeral moment of satisfaction which, if we're after a human equivalent to describe it, might feel something like the temporary achievement of an objective, that of remaining alive. But in a zoo, there's a lack of goals. To survive the absurdity of their existence, every captive must invent specific goals and expend all their energy achieving them. From this perspective, it helps if they choose goals that are extremely challenging but not impossible. Maintaining captive creatures in a satisfactory physical and moral state depends on their capacity to focus on the future.

The main character in *Wally Gator*, one of the cartoons that you watch although you've really outgrown them, is forever trying to escape from his zoo. To do this, he walks determinedly on his back feet, exactly as if he were part of the human species, and strides proudly beneath a great banner that marks the establishment's boundary. From here he goes into hiding until, at the end of every episode, the zoo's guards recapture him. Your enjoyment is twofold and also somewhat ambivalent. You're happy about the alligator's temporary escape from his guardians but you're relieved, show after show, to see his bids for escape end in failure. Zoo animals must not be allowed to cut and run, nor must their masters' surveillance be found wanting. Otherwise there'd be no more stories to dream up in your head and you'd have to go into action.

During the dromedaries' moulting period, we decided to gather the great tufts of hair, and to bring in packs of frozen blood from the abattoirs. We scattered it all in the big cats' cages. Thanks to these novelties, the cats are doing much better, they've got new smells to discover, they're stimulated, active, they've got things to do.

Being well fed and well housed has the effect of numbing our senses.

Transport for the animals should be conceived so as to provide sufficient space for them to stand upright inside, in their natural postures. Containers and equipment must moreover leave enough space above the animals' heads to maintain a suitable quality of air for the species being transported, especially when inside sealed vessels. Lastly, they must be sufficiently robust to bear the animals' weight, to prevent them from escaping or falling, to withstand stress arising from the animals' movements, and to include rigid divisions capable of withstanding any agitation among the animals which, for a range of reasons, from fury to incomprehension, have a tendency to throw themselves violently against their enclosures.

In the bathroom, in your bedroom, everywhere else, your body is changing in your absence. You've no means of seeing your evolving height, your features, your shape; your pauses at the mirror are closely monitored. You have a feeling that the space allowed you is shrinking year by year, though it's only that your limbs are growing.

In 2008, the Vincennes menagerie closed down. Its dilapidated facilities were crying out for renovation. They'd already overhauled the artificial Monkey Rock, a tall and extensive yet completely hollow cement-and-concrete structure which overlooked the whole zoo and was, in a way, the iconic attraction's signature, but the rest was unreformed. They had to move all the animals out, find them new homes, transport them in specially fitted lorries, ships and aeroplanes. They were sent to Paris-Le Bourget Airport in wooden boxes, destined for Algeria, except the giraffes, which were too complicated to move, and the two hippopotamuses, which refused to leave. Yet we had prepared them for their departure by making them climb into the boxes every day. We wanted to avoid anaesthesia, which carries risks and substantially adds to the animals' weight. But when D-Day came round, the female hippo panicked and started headbutting the bars. The male copied her and also became agitated. With the repeated blows and the animals' combined weight, the boxes looked close to breaking, so we had to give up on moving them.

We can imagine the lives those giraffes and hippos lead now, builders' cranes and rubbish skips their sole remaining company, awaiting as they are the new facilities through which their lives may come a little closer to those they had in the wild – at least for those that can remember it. Most of the animals were actually born in captivity and know nothing of the African savannah.

Your sense of your own body is much vaguer than your sense of some animals' bodies. Yet your mother has given you a book about the technical aspects of sexual relations, those relations being strictly limited to penetration. You've no wish to be penetrated, especially as, at least in this book, no link is made between penetration and pleasure.

Since the state refused to finance the zoo's renovation, an invitation for tender has been widely disseminated, yet businesses are proving slow to throw their hats in to shoulder the enormous cost of renovating an institution rumoured to be unprofitable even once renovated. The only hope to motivate private investment would be if a president were to take up the cause and, following the example of the primitive arts museum, the Museum of Modern Art and the National Library, decide to lend their name to this building site.

In the films you watch on TV with your parents, when the boys put their bodies on top of the girls, who are as a rule much younger, they almost all put their hand over the girl's mouth as if to stop her from speaking or shouting. You ask your mother what this gesture means. She explains that the girls are going to lose their virginity. You conclude that losing one's virginity leads to shouts that boys would rather not hear.

Now, we have no right whatsoever to buy and sell animals, but not so long ago it was easy enough to start a zoo, you went to a vendor who you informed exactly what you were after, and he made sure to provide it. As an anti-trafficking measure, wild animals no longer have value on the open market, yet many specimens still reach us through customs; they're seized as smuggled goods, the law requires that we receive them as such. When we have 250 snakes and a few crocodiles come through, as happened most recently, considering our space it's not always easy, and then we're criticised for the way we present the animals, their lack of accommodation or room to move around, but we're an official state museum, we're legally bound to provide this service.

To the advice you're given, to the requests you receive, to the hopes vested in you and that remain unspoken, you respond as loyally as you can. But your loyalty comes at a cost, so you compensate with mild exasperation, a degree of passivity and a good deal of inertia. Your body goes on changing.

Like at the circus, the zoo's audience is divided between the fear of seeing and the desire to see a handler be devoured alive by predators. This is why they crowd outside the windows or bars as soon as a human form penetrates the area reserved for the animals, penetration which is strictly regulated and, as of a few years ago, practically off limits both for security reasons and to avoid what is known as imprinting.

Your mother goes back to the art of cinema. You go with her to see the original version of *King Kong*.

If we want an orangutan to remain an orangutan we must interfere as little as possible, otherwise we humanise it. Yes, it's a little frustrating for the handler because they lose all direct contact with the animals, but rules are rules: we don't go into the cages, we don't try to tame them, we keep space between us. They must not forget where they're from and what they are.

If you were a monkey, if you were in captivity, if you knew that you'd never leave again, you might perhaps like us to remind you of your ancestors' story, but after a while, rather than maintaining a purposeless readiness for rebellion solely meant to reassure humans of their own good intentions, you might prefer to forget a past whose only use now is to gauge what you've lost. You'd prefer to be humanised. To be less unhappy, we become our own betrayers.

King Kong portrays our fantasised connection with animals, a tangle of revulsion, desire, fear and fascination all at once. The gorilla is much too big and too strong to live in our world; we must eliminate the gorilla. But by eliminating it, we find we are also eliminating part of our own story, our roots, and we are sad to see that great hairy body crumpled at the foot of the Empire State Building.

One day, a young orangutan came in straight from customs without any female to feed him. Of course at the nursery we loved feeding him and watching him grow, and as the rules weren't so strict at the time I even thought of taking him home and of my wife and me bringing him up. The hardest part was teaching him to climb trees and swing from them, at first he was always falling, we had no training for this and weren't always able to catch him when he slipped.

The problem with *King Kong* is you're not sure if you're meant to identify with the blonde girl who is, by the by, in one memorable scene patiently stripped to near-nudity by the creature, or with the young lover who saves her from the gorilla's vast grip, or with the gorilla himself, transformed as he is into a fairground attraction and bound by great chains to a scaffold taller than him. You don't dare ask your mother about the function of identification in the art of cinema.

The declared objective of wildlife parks is to preserve species as they are and ultimately to enable their reintroduction into the wild. We must therefore maintain the animals' natural instincts, recreate their former lifestyles while they're in captivity, teach them to identify with their own species, avoid raising them in close proximity to people. We must nonetheless recognise that in the majority of cases captivity has direct and irreversible consequences for the animals' behaviour.

We may infer many things about ourselves and our sexual identity from the character in *King Kong* – the blonde, the lover or the gorilla who ravishes women – with whom, without actually admitting it to ourselves, we identify.

Despite the crude nature of the special effects used in the 1930s to animate the beast, you identify with the gorilla. You don't say a word to your mother. To lie, you'd have to speak.

Imprinting consists of getting a wild animal used to a human presence as early as possible by hand-feeding it. The animal will take its feeder for its mother, it will fix on the image of the species which has raised it, and it will consider itself a human. If we then make it rejoin its fellow creatures, it will struggle to concede the similarity between itself and them and will consider them to be strangers or, worse, enemies.

You get used to leaving your bedroom unlocked, you don't even feel the old desperation to lock the door. You recognise that your mother is your mother, and your father is your rival and enemy, you reproduce the patterns, you embed the functions, you are imprinting.

Every time a new *King Kong* comes out, the special effects do more, so that the creature, reduced to a puppet in the earlier films, gains in psychological complexity with every remake. As the real animals disappear, the cinema offers us ever more ambitious, moving and almost human substitutes. The gorilla's humanity is the sign of its dying out.

You don't necessarily like people who go crazy for blondes, much less people who ravish women. But when the ravisher is a gorilla, you are guilty of lenience.

The animals must maintain their psychological well-being since, being required for intensive reproduction, to restock the wilderness, they have to hang on to some aspects of their past, we mustn't let them lose touch with everything. We wean the mammals slightly early so that the females come into heat again sooner, we remove that obstacle because we know that while they're looking after the babies they won't fall pregnant again, we just move on a bit faster, we save time so as to get better results and more specimens.

The handler has become an animal breeder. He separates the mothers from their young, not for any psychological benefit but in line with the requirements of profitability. It's as good as proven that motherhood is prejudicial to sex drive.

You stop observing yourself altogether, you have no wish to look at yourself in the mirror nor to see your body change, you assume the constraint, you don't like partners of your own species, you are imprinting.

Restocking nature with wild animals demands that we breed them before they become extinct but the breeding process considerably transforms the specimens and can sometimes make reproduction, learning and knowledge transmission extremely difficult. We are condemned either to the ongoing disappearance of species, or to the introduction of captive-bred bears, panthers and elephants fated to remind our descendants of some of the aspects of life in the wild that we have lost. Living animals will soon become museum pieces.

Once, when everything is going swimmingly and your parents already consider you a model adolescent, you rebel. From this occasion, you learn that it's much more effective to impose your will by means of discreet but deep-rooted resistance than by a raised voice and anger. You are imprinting.

A female orangutan will live with her mother up to the age of five and stays close until she is six or seven, when she first falls pregnant. She will not leave her mother completely until she has learnt how to give birth and how to nurse. If the chain of learning and imitation is broken, the female orangutan will not know how to raise her young. She will expel her infants without understanding, will take no interest in them and, without human intervention, the baby orangutans will starve to death, crying pitifully. We feed them by bottle while the mother looks on, hoping that this repeated gesture from behind a protective window will function as a lesson, as a historical trace and a reminder to the female, who's been deprived of her own mother and recreates the privation by leaving her newborn to itself.

You hope you won't have to stay with your mother until the birth of your first child. At the same time, you do nothing to make things change. You only leave your room for meals. You still don't lock your door, you make sure all your gestures are perfectly controlled and your behaviour is irreproachable. No one visits you. Only family enters your territory. You are imprinting.

As I wasn't managing to teach the female orangutan to look after her little one after the birth, I suggested showing her films of another female nursing her newborn. I even thought of leaving her to turn on the TV, so she could decide when she was ready to watch the looped programme we set up for her. It was entirely possible, we've already tried this with chimps turning on radios and even, if there's a poor signal, twiddling the dial until the voice is clearly audible. For monkeys just as for humans, cinema, radio and television can help with learning.

After meals, you stay to watch TV with your parents. You let them choose the programmes, which you watch without any impulse to assess their quality. You intensify your passivity. Slowly but surely, you are imprinting.

Despite the techniques of reintroduction into the wild and gradual liberation, as trialled by researchers, imprinted animals will have great difficulty adapting to the once-natural environment; they may seek sexual partners that aren't among their own species and, once they've reached sexual maturity, will tend at times of reproductive activity to attack humans, whom they'll view not as dangerous outsiders but as rivals.

Up to the age of sixteen you never go to the cinema without your mother. You keep boys at a distance. You have few friends. You rarely leave the family circle. You are imprinted.

I've had thirty-five years of life shared with that female, that's rare even among humans. So, when a problem came up, when they had to give her some medicine because she hadn't shat for a week, it was me they called. I opened the door, I went in, I gave her her medicine on a spoon, you get a little adrenaline buzz, this was after all the same lady orangutan who bit off one vet's finger and twice bit her handlers really badly, but she and I know each other well and we have mutual respect.

The more dangerous the animal seems, the more we respect it. Respect for the other is a means of pacifying the world, particularly when the other is already estranged. Offering the other the impression of equality is an excellent device for taking control.

Once you've understood that your bedroom door will stay unlocked for ever, that your childish games have had their day, that you will never be off with the reindeer after Christmas, that the cinema is a temporary release, that you love your mother too much, that no other human being can find favour in your eyes, that you cannot talk to anyone, that your family is protecting you, that you don't want it to protect you but you want to be protected, that you'd like to lock your bedroom door but aren't able to, you view the world with a degree of sorrow.

Now and then they get sulky, even if you enjoy looking after them they can take against you, they think of you as their jailer, with the big monkeys it's dreadful, they scream, they hit out in all directions, as they can't actually reach you, they've learnt how to spit on you.

Every response is natural. The animal cannot speak but it responds, there's an animal kind of response. Most of the time you don't respond, you develop and refine your use of silence. You await your moment.

We've just succeeded in breeding two northern tiger cats in captivity. It's been extremely difficult because they're solitary animals, they don't like to couple up at all, in the wild they mate and then separate immediately. We had to calculate when the females would be in heat practically to the hour, otherwise, when we tried putting a female in the cage with a male, he would kill her and in the morning all we'd have was a corpse. We had to find another solution. We brought up two little ones together, a male and a female, they got used to each other and when they were full-grown we left them together in the cage and they reproduced. They're the first cohabiting tiger cat couple on record, the first to raise their young together.

Naturally, I have to wonder if these two little cats brought up together mightn't be from the same litter.

And I hark back to the good old days when the male used to devour the female.

You don't know if your imprinting is a relief or a burden. You swing between resisting and going with it, you develop reflexes, you avoid excessively strong reactions, you are imprinted.

Recently, we've had to split our monkey collection in two because of aggression between the males. Knowing that there'll be roughly a 10 per cent turnover in a given year, we have to be ready to manage the population. As there's no more space, we've decided to sterilise them. We inject the males with hormone implants which should kick in over the next few days, the only risk is that this modifies the behaviour of the dominant male, that a sub-adult will usurp him and the hierarchy of the whole group will be turned upside down.

Human intervention could eliminate the role of dominant male altogether. One wonders why implants are not more systematically used for human contraception.

Once, you tried to belong to someone who wasn't your mother.

The reintroduction into the wild of wild species raised in captivity was envisaged for the purpose of species conservation, but it can also benefit commerce and the leisure industry. By releasing into a natural environment specimens that have only known captivity, we can for example benefit hunting, by increasing hunters' safety and their chances of success. Hunters know precisely the area where their prey has been released and this area can sometimes be enclosed in order to prevent the animals' escape. To further increase the hunters' chances of success, we sometimes medicate their prey prior to release. In any case, their life in captivity has enabled imprinting and their familiarisation with a human presence, such that the moment the rifle-toting marksman emerges from his hide, these former predators are without the fight-or-flight reflex. Thus, the marksman can experience the joy of the hunt without the usual concomitant inconveniences.

To find the person you'd like to take into your bedroom, you will have to get about a bit, learn patience, cunning, methods of approach, capture and grip. You are a novice in this domain.

Researchers have succeeded in perfecting artificial insemination techniques for some wild animals. This avoids their having to take specimens out of their natural habitats for the trials and studies they hope to realise. There are, for example, vast farms of bustards, a bird that has all but died out in Europe. Mostly located in Morocco, these farms produce around 100,000 specimens a year. Once they've hatched, the young bustards are taken to temperate regions where, over a precise and strictly regulated period, they become the highlight of the hunting season. Thanks to science, the hunt is no longer endangered.

Your first attempt to escape your mother lasts exactly eighteen months. During this time, you assiduously frequent a young man of the same age who was adopted at twelve and is unlikely to see his biological parents ever again.

By definition, wild animals belong to no one. Nonetheless, they can be acquired, under particular circumstances. For instance, it is possible, with special authorisation, to keep, to transport and to make use of birds of prey for hawking parties. For each bird, authorisation takes the form of a card that's reauthorised annually and that, in addition to the beneficiary's identity, provides data identifying the bird concerned.

A human has a right to an identity, a bird to an identification. The legal terms mark the distinction between humans and animals.

The young man you're seeing does not speak very good French and he's forgotten his mother tongue. When he receives letters from his mother, he can't decipher what she's written and he doesn't dare ask for help to translate them. You aren't any use to him, you can't translate the letters, you don't speak his mother's language. On the other hand, you speak your own very well and use it with a consistency and regularity that are unshakeable.

Banned throughout the territory: the mutilation, destruction, capture, removal or naturalisation of the common hamster, wolves, European lynx and bears; likewise their transport, resale, indeed any sale or purchase, whether living or deceased.

Every law is bound to recall the principles of separation and distinction at the origin of creation, to attenuate their implicit violence, to delimit precisely our gestures of defence, fury and control, to rebuild the barriers between species by situating beneficiaries on one side and violators on the other.

Your affection for the young man is growing, soon you'll invite him into your bedroom and face the risk of seeing your door open the moment that your body touches his. Concentrating so hard on that moment and that risk, you forget that this coming together is above all meant to bring you pleasure.

Imports are banned under all customs regimes, except for direct cross-border transits where there has been no change of authority or of the regime overseeing active progress, also the resale, advertisement for sale, sale or purchase of all non-domestic species of birds considered as game and the hunting of which is permitted. These regulations are applicable equally to the products arising from these species, notably to pâtés and preserves, as well as to their nests and their eggs. With temporary effect, the importation under all customs regimes of the common blackbird (*Turdus merula*) and thrush (*Turdus pilaris*) is permitted either fresh or frozen.

The young man with whom you'd like to lock yourself in your bedroom doesn't get on with his adoptive family. While he's losing touch with his native country's language, he finds that two of his cousins have moved to live near Paris, he calls them, sees them increasingly often and relearns to read his mother's letters. You continue to express yourself in French but your words sound like a foreign language to him.

We trap animals less and less, so it's harder to learn how to do it. It used to be twice a week for the monkeys, now it's twice a year, my expert touch has got a bit rusty. Netting them up is still OK but getting them to stay put is another kettle of fish. We have to hold them down, we're no cowboys, though there's still a buzz when we're prepping for some up-close and personal, we're jumpier than we used to be.

You try to belong to the young man you love but instead of being ruled by him as you'd hoped, you start ordering him around. You continue not locking yourself in your room and now you hate yourself.

You carefully conceal the existence of this young man you love from your parents, you conceal his origins and your connection to him. You have an idea that silence is your only place of freedom.

In the Pyrenees, cattle farmers do not practise trapping, they hunt and shoot wolves – in spite of the ban; when they land one, they hang him up in full view on an outcrop and if the other wolves want to go on tucking into goats and sheep, the farmers repeat the operation until they triumph through intimidation.

We don't know if wolves understand examples the way we do, but one thing's clear: picturing our own dead body swinging in the moonlight on the end of a rope is guaranteed to put us in a cold sweat, us humans at least.

You would like to be someone else but you don't know how to go about it. As for being yourself, that's an undertaking that feels beyond your powers.

It's illegal to keep a stun gun at home, it's a sixth-category weapon, so in the beginning we teach ourselves by practising on straw bales and polystyrene boxes. As we're shooting syringes, even though it's just compressed air, it's best not to miss the target, and that's not easy because the trajectory is parabolic and the animal we're aiming at is usually right in the middle of the troupe.

You try to contain yourself, to show as little as possible, to be perfectly smooth, to offer no holds. It's the first time in your life that you really love someone who isn't your mother.

Before, we didn't know how to anaesthetise animals, we didn't know the doses. If we wanted to look after the lion we had to force it into a trap, a kind of box, and as it wouldn't want to go in, we had to trick it, we'd frighten it, put some treats at the back, and as soon as it went in, bam, we'd close the trap behind it, the boxes had movable sides, we'd slide them in little by little until it couldn't move a whisker, then we'd inject it through the bars, it wasn't nice, it was completely terrified.

The young man you're seeing leaves his adoptive family without warning. You go several days without news of him. Your anxiety grows and betrays you. You love him. You explain your feelings to your mother, who is less than thrilled about your falling for such an exotic boy. You must choose between her and him.

Restraint and capture are the most delicate moments. If it's a python, a five-metre monster of 80 kilos, we have to be extra careful, we wallop him on the back of the head, he'll try to coil up straight away and if we let him he could well crush our bones or suffocate one of us, so we go in there four- or five-strong and we hold him a man per metre so he's got no chance of squishing us.

The young man you love moves into a room above a restaurant by himself. He does not give you his new address, and he's cleaning dishes instead of finishing school. It takes you some time to track him down and when you do, you realise he was trying to escape you.

If it's a crane, we take it *manu militari* and wear goggles, because when we pick them up they go for the eyes. For birds of prey and other birds, we use landing nets, there are five or six options depending on the size and weight of the creature, we get the bird in there and swipe it to the ground.

The young man you're now sure you love is avoiding you. You try everything to get back with him. You are not persuasive enough and besides, you're being watched.

We also used to practise containment by netting for the monkeys. But since they've been shown to carry diseases extremely similar to human ones, broadly since HIV, we don't go near them without gloves, we avoid net-trapping and use systematic stunning instead.

Thanks to the handler, you discover that identifying with a giant gorilla is not a biological nonsense. You feel ready to watch *King Kong* again with the young man you love, you suggest it to him, but he prefers new cinema to old.

Avian flu forced us to vaccinate all the birds in our aviaries. Three hundred and sixty birds representing over eighty species had to be captured several times over. Blood tests, the vaccine proper and booster shots were delivered in record time. We split into two teams and we went for the vultures, the birds of prey and the flamingos by hand. We became capture experts once again but there were a few glitches in the beginning. We caught our flock of forty flamingos, they had big webbed feet, we had to hold them by the necks while keeping their wings down, I must have held one of mine too tightly at one point, I heard a crack, it was a wing going. I'd bust one of my own birds' wings. When a flamingo has a broken wing, there's nothing you can do, you have to euthanise. I took three days to get over it.

Your relationship with the young man is close to an end. You aren't able to free yourself. You are fragile, vulnerable, unable to live in harmony with your fellow humans outside the family circle. Your imprinting has had irreversible effects.

You know there's little chance of your parents coming into your bedroom at night. Even while not locking your door for fear of having to explain why, you have time to think how life might be if your parents were dead. You think about your parents' deaths. You imagine the feelings you'd experience, the maze of steps to take, gestures to make, new things you'd have to learn. You don't know if you are despondent at the very idea of these deaths, their unavoidable nature, or if your despondency comes more from feeling that you're not ready, at your age, to handle the dizzying consequences. You aren't yet ready for your parents to die.

At the menagerie, we have a tortoise who's about 140, she must be the oldest tortoise in the world now, she weighs 250 kilos. She has huge scientific and sentimental value, and when she dies, hopefully a long time away still, they'll put in *The Guinness Book of Records* that a tortoise can live that long, more than 140 years, would you believe it.

You struggle with yourself and try to put your best foot forward. But when the young man you love suggests spending a little time in his bedroom, above the restaurant where he washes dishes, you come up with a thousand reasons not to go. As he persists, you give in, you go to his place, you exchange awkward caresses with your lover, you are self-conscious, you have no intuition, no flow, you have no sense of physical love. You are imprinted.

One of the primary ethical criteria for choosing a method of euthanasia (a key element for a good death) is the early-stage suppression of the central nervous system, which ensures immediate insensibility to pain and must be followed by cardiac and respiratory arrest. This is why we often recommend pharmaceutical methods. However, the use of pharmaceutical products demands guaranteed efficient disposal of the contaminated carcass.

Once again, the young man you love slips away from you. You can't sleep, you can't read, you've stopped eating, you avoid the TV programmes you used to watch for their anaesthetic properties, you blame your parents, you miss the time when you could imagine escaping with the reindeer after Christmas. You can't think of any way to escape. You are imprinted.

The acceptability of this or that method of euthanasia comes down to both the effective functioning of the equipment used and the competence of the person in charge. Cervical dislocation is acceptable in small rodents. It avoids chemical contamination of the tissues, requires no special equipment and leads to very rapid loss of consciousness in the subject.

In June, the young man you love hangs himself. You find out from one of your classmates. For several weeks, you say nothing to your parents. You don't want to see relief in their faces.

The most powerful image that's stayed with me is of the elephant's death, in 1976, a year and a half after I got here. I looked after him, I accompanied him and we helped him to die because he was suffering appallingly, he couldn't walk any more. One evening, we gave him a stun shot to put him to sleep, then we injected a drug with the syringe, we had to give him a litre of it. When we came back the next day to take him away, before the place opened, it was still dark, there he was, sitting up, leaning on the bars, like when they get up on stools in the circus, he'd died sitting up, I'll never get that image out of my mind, it's etched in there and will stay with me for ever.

When you tell your mother the bad news, she takes you in her arms, hoping to console you. You reject her embrace.

We have farms of rabbits, mice, guinea pigs and insects here. We breed them, and when we need them for our animals, we kill them. It never bothered me at all to feed live prey to the predators we keep here but it's not done like that any more. We have to kill them. We have a kind of gas chamber. We wouldn't call it that because it's nothing really, just a box we put the rats in and when it's ready we connect the tube, turn on the gas, count to fifteen, wait, when they're not moving any more they're done, we take them out.

Little by little, you get back in the habit of going to the cinema with your mother. You let her choose the film, the day, the time and the theatre, you express no opinion, you're not thrilled, nor needled, nor moved, you don't comment, it's your way of taking revenge. You aren't really there.

Carbon monoxide (CO) is a colourless, odourless gas and difficult to detect. Prominent in the waste gases produced by combustion motors, it contains impurities and can be harmful to animals and humans exposed to it. Although the animals to whom we administer it don't appear distressed, we prefer to use carbon dioxide (CO_2), which is non-explosive and easily sourced. Nonetheless, the concentration needs to be precisely controlled to ensure its anaesthetic effect. In fact, at low concentrations, carbon dioxide gas increases the breathing rate and causes respiratory distress. At 40 per cent concentration, it induces a slow-manifesting anaesthesia with a degree of agitation. It does not suit species that hold their breath (diving animals) or those with low respiration rates (amphibians and reptiles). Nor it is recommended for newborns that have survived pre-birth circumstances involving low oxygen concentrations. For this reason, newborn animals must be left in carbon dioxide units for at least half an hour after all movement has ceased.

At first your mother chooses children's films, as if that could alleviate your teenage-girl growing pains. You see *Dersu Uzala*, the tale of a trapper who lives alone in the taiga, on the Sino-Siberian border. You recall the time when you thought you could follow the reindeer after Christmas, you realise you wouldn't have been able to go by yourself, that nature demands skill and cunning, you feel more dependent even than you were as a child, your imagination is less fertile, your determination reduced, your defiance wearing thin. You take revenge in silence. You are not there.

We are shocked by the deaths of rats and mice but when we offer earthworms, snails, even fish to the menagerie's animals, it doesn't occur to any of us that this could be ethically dubious, as they can be prey and food just like the rest.

You still go on holiday with your parents instead of organising trips with friends your own age. In any case, you don't have school friends. You go with your parents, you eat with them, you visit the sites they visit, you swim where they swim. In spite or because of your docility, you discomfit the people your parents meet and with whom they'd like to chat. You are opaque, closed off. You take revenge through inertia and silence. You are not present.

Occasionally, animal liberation activist groups break into wildlife parks or demonstrate close by. On 15 June 2009 in Nantes, a dozen people, faces hidden behind crude dog masks, broke in close to where wolves were living in temporary accommodation. The group littered the building with leaflets which read: 'We're back. Don't think our dreams will be crushed like this. You thought you'd get around it but it catches up with you, it grips you by the neck. The drawbridge is raised but the walls are cracked.' The text is threatening, the tension between the we and the you pointed, even though at the end they acknowledge that we're all in the same boat. We thank the team but it's something we already had on our radar.

Usually, your mother chooses films that keep well away from sex, death and life's suffering, but sometimes she makes a bad call. After *King Kong*, *La Fête Sauvage* and *Dersu Uzala*, you watch Patrice Chéreau's *The Wounded Man*, a fresh way to discover sexuality: in the public toilets at the Gare du Nord. Doubtless a mistake on your mother's part; she can't have read the plot summary properly before taking you. You don't comment on what you're seeing as you sit beside her, you're learning that you can be simultaneously together and apart.

Whoever chooses to keep a large snake in their home must plan to provide the prey it will need to live on. Mice and rats are the recommended food, mice and rats which can readily be bought frozen for this purpose. A microwave must never be used to defrost the prey. For every meal, one of the bodies must be taken from the freezer and sat in a container of warm water. A pinky will defrost in two to three minutes, an adult rat may take a good two hours. To be sure that the defrosting is effective, you have only to feel the rat. If a sensation of cold or stiffness persists when you hold it in your hand, the warm-water immersion has not been long enough. The defrosted rodent should then be given a few seconds under an incandescent lamp to warm immediately before the meal. It is recommended that you wipe the rat with a napkin to remove excess water from its fur. For a snake to accept it, the defrosted rat must be as close as possible to the body temperature of a living rat.

Only much later do you see a film that definitively enlightens you about your own sexuality, a black-and-white film that's mysterious, dazzling, intriguing and poignant.

You devote yourself to studying and don't pronounce another word about the young man you loved, don't mention his name or reread his letters, you go on as if these events had no impact on your life, made no difference to your future. You are hardly there.

To give a newborn chick a good start, you have to feed it on newborn baby rats. We get the baby rats from the farm and have them minced. It's not the best in the morning on an empty stomach, but we do what we have to do. I'm not a vegetarian and my opinion is that if I'm going to eat meat, I have to deserve it, I have to be capable of killing an animal and butchering it.

In the evenings, you dine with your parents, showing no particular emotion and not feeling any. You learn how to be both together and alone. You are testing out numbness. You are hardly there.

We try through recruitment to even out the distribution of phobias, those who won't touch snakes, those who are afraid of spiders, those who can't put the rats in the box, those who can't bring themselves to mince them. Some people refuse to do it. You can't force them.

Your dazed state is temporary, at least that's what your parents think, what everyone thinks, what you also think. You are hardly there.

Before, when I was working down south, there was a fridge van which used to stop at a motorway service station just before Toulon, and which supplied all the zoos and circuses in the region. They had a contract with the abattoirs and collected the chickens, cows' hindquarters, the offal. I remember the spectacle of the pickups that used to stop there, in the middle of nowhere, to collect their meat, it was surreal.

You feel nothing, you think nothing, you're sleep-walking through life, you feel free, you feel alone, as if you're above the rest, ahead of the pack, you can't feel anything, you're detached, you hold yourself apart, you eat, sleep, study, you are calm and poised, you are sensible, you don't talk, you don't cry, you don't suffer, you don't make threats, you don't get angry, you're preparing yourself for a smooth and painless integration into the grown-up world. Slowly you are learning that you can be together and alone.

Here, luckily, we have a specialist company which sells us boxes of frozen spring chickens. It's a place that prepares everything zoos require, the handlers don't personally have to cut up meat that's been salvaged from abattoirs and declared unfit for humans, they can order from this wholesaler, and the dead rats, mice, chickens and processed meatballs can all be bought from this company.

You don't flinch, you don't sigh or grumble, you read, you write, you fill pages of notebooks, you pass tests and competitive exams, you study without striving, you are a step aside, behind, on the edge, you are vague, you're light, indefinable, casual, you move through life as if it were a cloud, a fine mist, a gauzy, insubstantial material, you live like a sleepwalker, you are anaesthetised, numb, you're dazed, nothing can rouse you. You learn that you can be together and alone. You're hardly there.

Ophidiophobia, musophobia, ornithophobia and arachnophobia are specific phobias defined by psychoanalysis as phenomena of projection and displacement. Instead of focusing on a significant object of love or hate (the father), the subject displaces their feelings onto a less significant object (rats, spiders, snakes).

Whatever the relationship between a handler and their parents, they must be able to capture a recalcitrant snake, to return a spider to its terrarium or to defrost chicks to feed young birds of prey. This is precisely the therapy that behaviourists recommend: the patient should be offered gradually increased exposure to the object of fear. The problem at the zoo is that it's difficult to organise the animals' care so that it aligns with the staff's therapeutic treatments.

You discover that, contrary to what specialists on animals in captivity say, boredom is not worse than death. It constitutes a slow version of it, the slow measure of time that we cannot use because we haven't learnt to think for ourselves, act for ourselves, feel for ourselves, suffer for ourselves, live for ourselves. We are bored when we've no independence and see no means to achieve it. In captivity, the imagination dries up.

You like animals but after a while you stop thinking about them, you stop demanding a living, furry, faithful companion, you stop directing your rage at your parents' refusal and the frustration it causes. You become used to not having what you want, or perhaps other, more troubling and deeper frustrations take over.

I am someone who's always had a good connection with animals, a kind of immediate instinct for animal feeling, and besides, I was very interested in natural science and how we understand life, so I chose to study biology, I've taken a classic path.

You used to think that people who work with animals don't talk about their love for them. You thought that love was only for those who didn't touch, had no experience of, had nothing to do with the use, breeding and butchering of animals. You used to think that love was a luxury, a pleasure solely available to those who admired animals from afar or who kept them as pets.

Having left school to begin higher education, you don't look back, nor do you keep up with the schoolmates you used to see. You choose to begin a brand-new life, to keep the old one to yourself, never to mention it, to engineer separate sections within you, between which communication is impossible, to divide, to distinguish, to break up.

The first contradiction is philosophical. We experiment on animals because they are like us, yet at the same time we consider them sufficiently different to use them in experiments. The second is personal: usually people like me do biology because they like animals and then the job makes us treat them as if we don't care. You have to get used to it. I've only belatedly started to question my practice, in the beginning I went for a very standard path.

The institution where you study is relatively far from your home. This allows you to establish some distance, develop some strategies for retreating, to build some protective barriers, some ditches, palisades, fortifications, ramparts. You retreat, you hide, you separate off, you fade out, you try out silence. You are preparing yourself.

Ethics are complicated because there's a very strong anthropomorphising tendency towards pets, yet at the same time, statistically, the number of animals used for experiments is very low compared to the numbers that we eat. In our lifetime, considering the complete range of research practices, it comes to about one and a half mice and half a rat.

Following the discovery of this data, I see my life unfold in the shape of a rodent cut in two, of which one half has been sacrificed for my health and the other for the health of someone close to me. If I die young, the number of animals used on my behalf could add up to a whole number. At least then I'd have the consolation of not being responsible for the systematic sectioning of lab rats.

You are spending more and more time far from home, you meet students with whom you go to cafés, you demonstrate in the streets, you argue, you debate, you read. But, even though you're convinced to the contrary, your distance makes no difference to the exclusivity of your relationship with your mother. You are contaminated.

In the animal research centres, the risks posed by the animals can be divided into two distinct groups. Either they come from animals that are themselves carriers of their own infections, which in some cases (known as zoonoses) are transmissible to humans. Or the risks arise from the manipulation and inoculation of laboratory animals that have been correctly cared for and are completely free of pathogens. Experimentation demands risk management. In fact, people assume a degree of risk that they must be able to measure when they inoculate animals with all kinds of fatal diseases.

Your feelings towards various young people in your circle are confused but, though you don't understand why, your body responds only partially to the ardent desires described to you and so often depicted in the books and films that you like. You feel alone, you feel out of step, you feel dazed, numb, ill at ease, sick, disabled. You are contaminated.

There are four categories of animal labs corresponding to the four groups of pathogens. Group 1 includes biological agents not known to provoke disease in humans. Group 2 includes biological agents which may pose a danger to humans but among which transmission by proximity is highly unlikely. Group 3 includes biological agents capable of causing serious illness in humans. Effective treatments or prophylactics are available but transmission in the community remains possible. Group 4 contains the most dangerous biological agents: those that cause serious illness, are highly transmissible and for which there is neither treatment, nor prophylaxis.

To succeed in pre-empting the dangers of contamination arising from the inoculation of lab animals with serious diseases, you must be certain that the mental and psychological barrier between people and animals is impregnable. And wherever it may not be impregnable, the means for making it so must be found.

Your body and your mind live two parallel lives. While your knowledge is flourishing and broadening, you continue in ignorance of your physical self. You are dazed, bewildered, unmindful, distracted, absent, deaf and blind. You are forgetting yourself.

We create models in the labs, for example models of obese mice, rats deprived of sugar, monkeys with Parkinson's or baboons with multiple sclerosis, but this doesn't mean that we're mistreating animals; we carry out surgery in exactly the same conditions as human surgery, we intubate them, we perform gaseous anaesthesia, we administer analgesics and antibiotics, we are very careful with our subjects insofar as, in order to obtain good scientific data, we must keep the animal in good health, have it awaken comfortably, without any suffering and infection-free; only under these conditions can its disease progress smoothly.

You too – your pathology is advancing smoothly but at no point do you feel that you're suffering from disease, from melancholy or from depression. You don't worry about what's happening to you, about the way you avoid everything that troubles you. You forget yourself.

You go to see Jacques Tourneur's film *Cat People* with friends your own age who, like you, enjoy old black-and-white American films. The film tells the story of a Serbian woman living in the US who meets a well-brought-up American and marries him. Seemingly a film you could easily have watched with your mother.

For each level of animal breeding centre (classified from A1 to A4), isolation facilities in line with contamination prevention standards must be provided. The isolation units are always located well away from other facilities. The isolation zone must be maintained under pressure with double airlock entrances and feedback-controlled doors. For levels A2 and A3 breeding centres, the isolation facilities are moreover indicated by a graphic depicting 'biological hazard'. Peepholes are provided in the doors to enable observation of isolation rooms. We must also allow for hermetic sealing of the accommodation for the purpose of post-occupation sanitisation.

On general release in 1942, Tourneur's *Cat People* opens with an image of a cage in which a magnificent

116

black panther paces ceaselessly from left to right and right to left. The first time you see the film, you don't understand what grips you, what attracts you to it. You watch without thinking, without responding. Nothing awakens you. You have ignored yourself for too long.

I began, as everyone does, by experimenting on decerebrated frogs. We decerebrated them ourselves, it's very quick, you insert a stylet into the back of the animal's neck and you cut out the brain. It's not nice but there's a whole lot of material out there justifying it, research standards demand it, these are good deeds, we're improving the human race. As I'm an elder sibling and psychological tests show that first-born children are much more conformist than second ones, well, I'm happy to go with the flow, I do what I'm told, I've taken a very classic path.

In Tourneur's *Cat People*, which you see without your mother, the main character Irena Dubrovna, played by Simone Simon, invites Mr Reed to have tea with her the first time they meet. It's highly inappropriate, you have to admit, but you can excuse a Serb for not knowing American ways. You see Mr Reed and Irena Dubrovna go up the stairs to the young woman's apartment. You expect Mr Reed's entry into the building to mark the beginning of their sexual relationship. You are wrong. Instead of the scene so impatiently awaited, in which, for example, Mr Reed takes the mysterious young woman in his arms – nothing. A dazzling ellipsis wrong-foots you.

Contamination between animals and humans is often more complex than we expect and if we don't take strict precautions, full-blown health crises may follow. For example, Aids began with people hunting in the bush, killing HIV-carrier chimps for food and being contaminated by the virus via scratches while cutting up the bushmeat. Just one illustration of how an epidemic of such proportions may begin with some very marginal event that we didn't think to avoid or to treat as such.

'Oh, I hadn't realised how dark it was getting,' says Irena Dubrovna in the next shot. You aren't sure if she's speaking to Mr Reed, there on the sofa, or to you, the viewer, sunk deep in your cushions and still thrilled, surprised, disappointed, almost outraged that the desire between Reed and Irena has not taken a tangible form. But in this film desire never takes a tangible form, or when it does, it's already too late. Unquestionably a film you could have seen with your mother, you think, and sigh.

In a lab-based animal breeding centre, the distinction enforced between the animals' pre-intervention lives (the dirty zone) and their lives during and post-intervention (the clean zone) is crucial in order to avoid the interference of food, urine, excrement, hairs, vomit, saliva or parasites with the results of any given experiment. Contamination protocol demands the establishment of exacting standards and the use of high-quality equipment. The slightest error puts staff safety at risk and, in the event of leaked pathogenic agents, threatens a proportion of the human race at large.

In *Cat People*'s second scene, sexual allusions come into focus. At last you decide that it's better, for the sake of dramatic tension and the film's high standards, for sex to remain at the level of discussion and for there to be no transition to the act. This is, of course, what your mother would have thought. You find yourself thinking like her. You're trapped. You must look for ways of freeing yourself. You are preparing.

Isolation is guaranteed by the use of almost completely sealed aerated enclosures. These enclosures, or biosafety cabinets, ensure the protection of the technician by means of a motor-driven suction point at the front of the work area, drawing air around the user and into the cabinet. Thus, biosafety cabinets provide an invisible barrier between technicians and their biological samples. Critically, they ensure the protection of samples from contamination by means of the vertically descending, unidirectional airflow that enters through their air filters. Contamination can equally arise from the lab environment and from other samples under examination at the same time.

In the regulation scientific terminology, the words 'sample', 'supplies' and 'equipment' may indicate either manufactured items, or living creatures reduced to the condition of guinea pigs.

During Reed's second visit to Irena, she, kneeling at the feet of her American friend, softly hums 'Dodo l'enfant do' to him, a lullaby more often employed to send babies to sleep than to arouse a lover. You conclude that she is muddling maternal love with another kind of love, one more appropriate to the two protagonists' ages and sexes. You realise that *Cat People* will not show you how to escape your mother.

The manuals on procedures for inoculating animals with pathogenic agents include descriptions of autoclave points, chemical safety valves, sterilisation procedures, equipment flow, clearance space, storage zones, clean zones, dirty zones, containment breaches and cleaning products. On the other hand, no mention at all is made of the animals used, neither in the texts, nor in the illustrations that usually run alongside them, as if the presence of living things might obstruct the functioning of an entirely mechanised, computerised, industrialised and dehumanised system.

Before marrying Mr Reed, Irena Dubrovna admits to her future spouse that she suffers from all kinds of fears and phobias which have been passed down from mother to daughter since time immemorial. One ancient legend from her country tells that if she sleeps with a man, she will turn into a panther. Irena feels torn between two irreconcilable desires: the desire to marry and the desire to remain faithful to her past. You feel like Irena Dubrovna, unable to decide. You are trapped.

The French Animal Rights League campaigns for animals' right to respect. According to this line of thought, the league proposes that we reshape scientific vocabulary so as to increase researchers' awareness of the ethical problems posed by experimenting on animals. The league calls for scientific publications to stop referring to animals under the classic heading 'equipment' but to create a new heading for them: 'biological subjects'.

I used to have a colleague who worked with cats, which is quite unusual. To investigate the influence of sense activity on their digestion, he fitted them with gastric cannulae and set them up on a sort of hammock. He'd lie them on their stomachs, their paws dangling over the worktop, then he'd stimulate them with pictures and odours, and gather the gastric juices through the cannulae, a working method that could well appear indefensible to the general public. Well, far from fearing the moment of being lined up on their hammocks, the cats in question used to fight to be first inside the lab. They knew that at the end of each experiment they'd get tasty things to eat.

We concoct a lot of mistaken ideas about animal experimenting; the nightmare visions we're peddled are often far from the truth. It's difficult to know if caged animals are content but many are much less stressed than in the wild: they've no predators, no anxiety about food, they are visibly healthier than if they'd been left to themselves.

For fear of incurring all kinds of reprimands, you follow your parents' recommendations to the letter. You never go to bed naked with a man in order not to fall pregnant; in order not to be attacked in the street you never come in after midnight: the night-time curfew fixed by your parents. The world is full of blind alleys and other perils. You are forgetting yourself.

In experiments inoculating lab animals with pathogenic agents, contamination by dermal contact can occur if the skin tissue is infected or damaged. This could be the case, for example, following animal scratches or bites, scrapes from contaminated glassware or even cuts from surgical instruments occasioned during procedures on living or dead animals.

Mr Reed does not believe his wife will turn into a panther and kill him. 'You're Irena. You're here in America. You're so normal you're even in love with me, Oliver Reed, a good plain Americano. You're so normal you're going to marry me. And those fairy tales: you can tell them to our children.' In 1942, no doubt the viewers hoped Irena would fall into line, get married and draw a line under her legacy of fear. You start to think like them. You no longer believe in fairy tales nor in the flight with the reindeer after Christmas. You try to calm down. You are forgetting yourself.

We practise conditioning on the monkeys. This means spending a three- to four-month period training the primates to pick up objects secreted in little grooves all over a board. They really enjoy this because the board is dotted with treats so they pick up the objects as quickly as they can. It's a hellish task, you have to train them every day, teach them to leave their cages by themselves, sit in the right chair of their own volition and stay there, aided by some kind of partial restraint, otherwise after five minutes they're scratching their arses and ambling off elsewhere.

Mr Reed ought to have been more cautious. He ought to have suspected that singing a lullaby to a man one claims to be in love with is not a healthy sign. But Mr Reed is a warm, open American, ready to kiss and to penetrate a pretty Serbian woman as soon as their marriage has been celebrated. Indeed, marriage provides for copulation with total impunity and the consent of all concerned; it constitutes an effective means of definitively curbing one's fantasies, giving them a more decorous, appropriate, more regular form, so as not to scare oneself. You support Mr Reed's decision, you don't want to be afraid, to stand out, to step out of line. You are forgetting yourself.

Once trained, the monkeys attain a maximum speed at completing the task. When this point is reached, we open a lesion in the cervical region of their spinal cord, a lesion which will modify the fine motor skills in one of their hands. Next, we observe how long it takes for the monkey to spontaneously recover its capacities by comparing the speed of execution in the wounded right hand and the undamaged left, bearing in mind that, unlike humans, monkeys are ambidextrous. After that, we may graft in therapeutic cells to see if recovery can be hastened.

Caring means finding the remedy to an illness that one has already deliberately introduced.

Having inculcated you with their fear of the other, your parents explain that you're too wild and urge you to be more sociable. To set you right, they are ready to connect you with their own selection of inoffensive and well-intentioned humans. You mostly refuse the therapy they're trying to prescribe. You are preparing.

When training mice, two reinforcements are used: positive and negative. Positive reinforcement consists of starving the mouse and only giving it a ball of food if it has correctly carried out the tasks we want it to carry out. Whereas for negative reinforcement, we use electric shocks to give the mouse an aversion to something. This is the principle of punishment and reward, of which we know that punishment is far more effective even though it's not at all nice to electrocute mice, sometimes the shocks are too powerful, they squeak, some die, they cling to the bars and channel the whole current, though it's worth saying that some are also a bit thick.

To avoid explanations, arguments, confrontations and collateral damage, you never disobey the rules established for you, sometimes you narrow their remit even further, so you can never be caught out. For example, not only do you never go naked in a boy's bed but you make sure never even to be alone and clothed in a boy's bedroom. You are forgetting yourself.

Conditioning means teaching a given animal to do what you want as if it were acting of its own accord – without your resorting to torture. It requires a long and difficult training phase which handlers generally much prefer to using blows and violent methods. No one wants to be the baddie.

You never step out of line, you come home at the agreed hours. Your obedience lulls your vigilant parents, you could easily take advantage of their confidence in you to betray them. You are preparing.

Some campaigning groups have decided to take action against the systematic incarceration of animals and people. On 27 June 2009 in Nantes, men dressed in black, their faces masked, broke into an area where some wolves were to be displayed. They broke glass and furniture, and sprayed liquid pitch over the floor and walls. They left after this violent intervention, shouting demands for the joint liberation of humans and animals. No detailed guidance was provided as to how we might carry out this double liberation.

As you watch *Cat People* unfold, you realise that a calm and ordered life would mean nothing to the main character. It might be better for her to show her claws and turn violently against all the sexual predators circling around her. You're plunged into confusion; you can't decide if you wish Irena Dubrovna would consummate her marriage to Mr Reed or if you'd prefer her to escape and turn into a wild animal. Your own uncertainty troubles you. You're afraid you may not be sufficiently conditioned. You are trying to control yourself.

Primates are very destructive animals. In the lab centres where they experiment on monkeys, the cages must have smooth walls, no handholds, and be able to withstand repeated washing with high-pressure sprays. Earthenware finish along the top of all walls and epoxy resin grouting fulfil these requirements.

As soon as the marriage has been celebrated, Mr Reed realises that the sexual relations he was counting on pursuing with his young wife remain in contention. Irena refuses him gently but firmly. Having hoped to watch torrid scenes between Reed and Irena, you now hope that the metamorphosis Irena is so afraid of will happen before the end of the film. Your expectations, your hopes, your desires have changed, despite your only partial awareness of this revolution. You are preparing.

The enclosures' floors, their gutters and waste pipes are made of washable materials. The porcelain tiles, flooring with a watertight underlay extensive enough to encase the joins, plinths with curved bases, treated surfaces with a 1 per cent slope towards stainless-steel drains are specially recommended for the evacuation of purine and residual water.

Every time Irena Dubrovna refuses her husband, Mr Reed's, advances, you are both sorry and relieved. Instinctively you know it's better not to talk about it, you continue to live in silence, dazed and blinkered, although this hardly prevents you from ringing changes, from seeing people your own age while taking care to be home on time every evening. You are holding back.

Thinking about suffering we imagine unbearable things, but it's worth knowing that you can pick up a rabbit, for example, a nervous creature, and lay it on its back – easily done when you've learnt to handle animals – and then you can stretch out its paws and do intracardiac blood taps, directly from the heart, without the slightest squeak or wriggle from the rabbit. You can't insert a needle into a human's heart without anaesthesia, the pain would be too intense, which goes to show that situations, reactions and physiologies aren't always comparable.

You're not in pain, you're not sad, you're not depressed or nostalgic or upset, you don't think about the young man you loved and who hanged himself in his bedroom, you move forward with the consistency of a metronome, a robot, an automaton, you've no awareness of your own emotions, you're not listening, there's no feedback, you are dazed, numb, deaf, blind. You are holding back.

I first worked with planarians. These are little flatworms which live under the rocks in unpolluted rivers. I'd ordered some from the United States but hadn't managed to get them through, they arrived dead, couldn't survive the journey, so I had to go and fish up some I could work with in French rivers, I made quite a splash among the locals with my waders and containers, I supplied my own animals, that's quite unusual but it's very handy, and as for reproduction, you just cut one planarian in half: now you have two.

You try not to think about death, you try not to think about desire, not to think about the link between the two; you eat, you sleep, you talk, you make jokes, you smile, you study with unfailing tenacity and regularity, nothing disturbs you, nothing stops you, nothing surprises you, nothing triumphs over you, nothing disarms you, nothing weakens you, you control everything, you monitor everything, you watch everything, you are holding back.

Animal welfare militants are behind a range of attacks targeting researchers at the University of California (UCLA) who do experiments on animals. In June 2006, a Molotov cocktail was thrown into a garden in Bel Air, Los Angeles. The arsonists hoping to damage the home of a UCLA psychiatrist had the wrong address. Luckily, no fire broke out. In June 2007, another Molotov was thrown at the car of a different researcher but the bomb did not explode. In October 2007, the house of a specialist on nicotine addiction was vandalised. In June 2008, a van belonging to UCLA was damaged by another home-made fire bomb. In November 2008, a vehicle was destroyed and two others seriously damaged during an attack organised by animal rights activists who claimed responsibility for the attack and said they'd been aiming at the house of a UCLA researcher whose experiments involved animals. The police stated that the activists had hit the wrong target. In California, animal rights militants are primed to carry out acts of violence but their equipment remains primitive; they could do with a few high-grade GPS links to improve their hit rate for those they claim to be aiming at.

'The cats torment me. I wake in the night and the tread of their feet whispers in my brain. I have no peace, for they are in me.' You endlessly repeat this line, spoken by Irena Dubrovna in *Cat People*. They are in me. And you know that everyone who sees the film can project into that pronoun 'they' all the powers that press down on them, that constrain and condition, and on which, despite their resistance or attempts to escape, they depend. You are suffocating.

Professor McConnell has shown that some acquired properties can be transmitted from one animal to another, even among invertebrates. For example, we can teach planarians to contract in response to light, conditioning them with electric shocks. Once they have acquired this property, we chop them up finely and serve them to other planarians to eat – and we observe that the cannibal planarians are much quicker at acquiring the property of contracting under light than the first, sacrificed planarian. From this we conclude that an acquired property is transmitted by ingestion of cell matter, in other words, by means of cannibalism.

Cat People has opened your eyes neither to the forces that hold you back, nor to the ways they act on you. You don't think about the young man whom you loved and who hanged himself in his bedroom, you are neither sad nor impassioned, neither furious nor exalted, you keep your distance from other people and from yourself, you don't listen to your emotions, you bury them, you stifle

131

them, you deny them. Although you've a feeling you'll have to leave your mother, you hold back.

Not all animals are equivalent. The vertebrates and the octopods are the most highly evolved: they have emotions. We aren't sure that insects have emotions, we don't know but we think they are genetic automata. What scientists can say is that an ant's life doesn't have the same meaning, even to others of its species, as that of a ram; there is a process of evolution towards indi-vidualisation, some animals are more individualised and have developed a limbic system, i.e. a nervous system capable of producing emotional perceptions. It's clear that the need for and meaning of individualisation for an earthworm are not the same as for a chimpanzee. There's a hierarchy that depends on the animals' mode of functioning as a species. Animal rights must take this hierarchy into account. In other words, it's not the same thing to tear the wings off a fly and to cut off a mammal's limbs.

Having identified with a gorilla that ravishes women, you now identify with Simone Simon, a foreigner who's afraid she's turning into a big cat. You are preparing.

The facilities for the animals' accommodation abso-lutely demand soundproofing, especially if the breeding centre is situated close to laboratories or to any other building where staff will be working. The animals can be noisy and all the more so when kept several to a cage.

In a moment of doubt and ambivalence, you feel as much a prisoner as the big cats, but your prison has no name, no depth, no extent, no volume, no odour, no ways in or out. As biologists say, the situation is anxiogenic.

We can create models to measure the link between anxiety and balance. To do this, the mouse must be made anxious, by being shut inside either an unlit box, or what's known as a rodent restrainer, a transparent container with small air holes, inside which a mouse cannot move at all. In this way, we can provide a given population of anxious mice. After letting them grow hungry, we send two populations of mice, the anxious ones and the rest, to walk on turning bars, knowing that if they succeed in walking along their bar they'll get a reward at the end. We have been able to show that the population of anxious mice will slip and fall from the bar whereas the population of unstressed mice will manage to walk right along the bar, as far as the ball of food.

Correcting natural injustice would really consist of giving food to the anxious mice in compensation for what we've just put them through. Scientific research demands suspension of judgement.

To show Irena how much he loves her, Mr Reed wants to give her a pet. He takes her into a small pet shop in town, the animals all become restless in their cages, they panic and howl as if something were threatening to kill them. When Irena leaves the shop, the animals immediately calm down. You are almost relieved:

Irena Dubrovna's metamorphosis into a big cat must be imminent.

We can do the same kind of experiment on rats as we did with the planarians. We train the rats to develop an aversion to darkness by a very simple method. We give them a choice between a transparent box and a dark, unlit box and every time they go into the dark box, we give them an electric shock. When the rat has acquired the aversion to darkness, we kill it, mince its brain and inject extracts from this into new rats. We observe that the injected rats acquire their aversion to darkness much more rapidly than their non-injected fellows. From this we conclude that there is a molecule that may be responsible for transmitting fear of the dark.

Biological research shows that we can isolate a range of molecular carriers of the fear of darkness, of the intention to contract, of anxiety or stress. We would hope that other molecules will lead to happier discoveries.

Irena Dubrovna is showing signs of weakness. Slipping her hand with its long, polished nails inside the cage of her little canary, a gift from her husband, Mr Reed, she accidentally kills it, whether by mistake or by instinct. It is doubtless this killer instinct that makes her feed her pet bird's body to the nearby zoo's black panther, which she visits and admires increasingly often and which paces relentlessly around its cage. You are almost relieved: Irena Dubrovna's metamorphosis into a big cat is imminent.

Foundational research sometimes allows us to make unexpected and game-changing discoveries. For example, a researcher working on canary song, trying to understand why some male canaries sing all year round while others only sing during their courtship displays, carried out a range of interventions and transplants on these two groups of canaries. He realised that following a courtship display, the canaries that sang intermittently showed significantly reduced neurones in the cortical region which regulates their song, and that during the subsequent courtship display a large number of neurones returned. Thus, he discovered that the cortex harbours a germinal zone, and that's how he was able to show the existence of stem cells. Research can take us much further than studying birdsong would suggest.

Irena Dubrovna is jealous. When she realises that her husband is staying a little too late at work with his colleague in the evenings, she cannot help but sneak into the office and, in a manner alien to her usual poise, to pursue, threaten, even attack the woman who risks usurping her place at her darling husband's side. You fervently hope that Irena will spare herself the pain of killing her rival. And that Mr Reed will be strong enough not to demand that his wife sleep with him. At the same time, you're almost relieved: Irena Dubrovna's metamorphosis into a big cat is imminent.

In California, the animal rights militants are growing more aggressive, more accurate and therefore more dangerous. On 22 April 2009, they went after J. David

Jentsch, who studies schizophrenia and drug addiction by experimenting on vervet monkeys. This time they managed to set fire to his Volvo, which was parked near his home in Westside, Los Angeles. Jentsch, who belongs to UCLA's 'Pro-Test' organisation, has stated that abandoning animal experimentation would be a disaster for research both pure and applied in the field of human healthcare. But when this scientist decided to take a stand, others refused to testify and laid low. The same happened to another UCLA researcher whose name we will not reveal, who, after months of harassment and threats, decided to give up his work for fear of reprisals and sent an email to the associations for animal liberation which read: you've won.

One evening, you forget the curfew when you absolutely have to be back home. You return after midnight, your parents are waiting for you on the doorstep. To calm their nerves, you point out that you haven't yet turned into a pumpkin.

When a chick is born, like all nidifugous birds, in the first hours of its life it must learn to follow its mother, otherwise it will be killed and eaten by birds of prey or foxes. This is what we call pursuit behaviour. In the labs, we've worked on imprinting, that is, on very early behaviour training. We've had chicks hatch in incubators, we slept on camp beds to be sure that we'd be there when they were born. Because you have to start working with them exactly sixteen hours after they hatch, otherwise it's too late. We teach them to follow moving coloured balloons rather than their mother. And we've shown that chicks injected with particular molecules learn more quickly than other chicks to substitute a balloon for their natural parent; in short, there are molecules that improve learning.

Despite your wish to escape the family fold, learning to follow bobbing balloons rather than your mother does not represent sufficient progress for you to submit to this kind of experiment. You need to find another trick to break away from your mother.

I should expand this imprinting narrative to include the aspect of sexual imprinting. On reaching adulthood, male chicks will seek their sexual partners among objects that resemble the object they followed in the very earliest stage of their development. Therefore, if we manoeuvre things such that a chick follows balloons instead of its mother, as an adult chicken it will prefer to partner with a balloon. From this finding, eminent psychoanalysts have been able to state that the same kind of behaviour can be found among men who sometimes seek to couple, not with their mother, exactly, but with a woman who resembles her.

This tells us nothing of the adult sexual lives of the female chicks and children who, in order to escape the threat of predators have, of course, just like their male counterparts, learnt to follow their mother.

Irena Dubrovna lives entirely alone in America. But now and then she happens to recognise a familiar face in a woman she comes across. Like everyone else in the cinema, you admire the strange and feline face of this passing woman on the screen, the intense gaze she directs at Irena, you listen to the strange, incomprehensible and seductive words she speaks to her, words with which she marks her and Irena's belonging to the diabolical world of panther-women. You are my sister, you are my sister, she says, in a language that sounds like Serbo-Croat or Moldovan. You read the translation that appears below the picture. You don't know if this declaration should be understood as good news or a terrible situation. Still, upon learning that there are several panther-women in the United States, you realise, without entirely understanding why, that instead of being terrified you are reassured. You are preparing.

In Tourneur's *Cat People*, you side not with Mr Reed, the disappointed and frustrated husband, but with Irena, you worry over *her* fears, her fear of coming to prey on the man she loves. Having identified first with a gorilla who ravishes women, you now identify with a woman who's prepared to eat men and who, for this reason, refuses to sleep with her lover. All in all, you haven't made much progress since *King Kong*. You even wonder if you may be regressing.

The improvement of animals' living conditions lies less in the experiments themselves than in what surrounds them. Animals must enjoy the best possible living conditions, they must eat well, drink well, be kept at the right temperature, the idea is that animals be treated optimally between experiments. Suppose for example that we wish to observe the effect of liver cancer upon glucose levels, we would have to cause the animal to have liver cancer and measure its glucose levels, we couldn't do otherwise, the experiment demands it. Nonetheless, we could ensure it dies comfortably.

You are convinced that science and scholarship demand sacrifice. You don't yet know of what, you will discover this little by little.

The word euthanasia appears repeatedly in texts on the use of animals. Yet, while its etymology suggests gentle death, it is more often applied, in current usage, to the act of provoking death in those desperate to put an end to their intolerable physical suffering. Although they don't expressly wish for it, animals may benefit from euthanasia. On the other hand, even if they express a keen wish for it, people are never accorded the right to such a treatment. Offering one's opinion therefore does no good at all, so it's better, as animals do, to stay dumb. To ensure zero confusion over the line between humans and animals, we are subject to horrifying inconsistencies.

Irena Dubrovna has no illusions about herself. The world she lives in was not made for her. You don't wish to be like her. And yet, when she's weeping in the bath because her first metamorphosis has actually happened, you weep too.

If, as a result of poor treatment or lack of care, captive animals are found to be seriously ill or injured or in a state of poor psychological health, the police commissioner can order that they be put down or euthanised on the spot.

At twenty-two, you meet a sweet, gentle young man who likes you. You agree to make love with him, you say very little, show as little as possible, continue your studies and remain beneath your parents' roof, where he is obliged to join you in order to embrace you once or twice a week.

When for whatever reason during transport the delivery of captive animals is delayed or interrupted, or if the relevant authority finds that the facilities in place for in-transit protection are insufficient, and should appropriate care measures not be possible to enforce, the police may order that the animals be put down on the spot.

I have occasionally saved rats and brought them home with me rather than leave them to some sticky end. Because it's never nice to kill things. You can soften the sting by deciding that humans would be happy to die in a few seconds like that, but it's not nice. And it's even harder when you're killing by means of a brain aneurysm instead of gassing them, even if you try thinking that it's much quicker than gas.

Killers spend the rest of the time trying to feel better about killing.

Your studies will go on for a long time. In order to stay with you, the mild and modest young man who would like to share your life is obliged to share your and your parents' roof. He asks you to move in with him. You delay the moment. Your metamorphosis is imminent.

Most of the physical methods allow us to kill animals without cruelty. Decapitation, for example, consists of separating the body from the head. Specially designed guillotines are required in order to carry this out. This method's advantage lies in the animal's rapid loss of consciousness. On the other hand, the procedure is aesthetically unpleasant and can cause injury to the handler.

Your desire for humanity is about equal to your desire to be animal. In fact, it's quite impossible to tell the two apart. You are afraid.

For younger or smaller animals with softer skulls, it can be acceptable to deliver a blow to the head. Then the animal's death must be confirmed. It is essential that the person in charge of the operation have the required training and skills for the act to be carried out without hesitation and very swiftly.

You envisage in the future settling down with the mild, modest and loving young man who lives with you at your parents' house. This gives you time to imagine how life might be as a wife and what you will become. You delay leaving home, you find excuses. Your metamorphosis is imminent. You are afraid.

Administered at a high enough concentration, all the inhalant anaesthetics in use today (halothane, isoflurane) may kill an animal. Tests (preferably carried out on rodents) show that the product these animals are least averse to is halothane. It has the advantages of being easily vaporised and causing little irritation upon inhalation. It must nonetheless be administered inside a sealed room so the gas can be evacuated without the handlers being exposed, for it is extremely toxic to humans.

You complete your studies. You have no further excuse not to leave the family home. Despite your efforts, you still don't know how one distinguishes and divides love from dependence. In your experience, the two are closely connected. You hope your metamorphosis is not far off. You are afraid.

Administered in high doses and intravenously, all derivatives of barbiturates tend to be excellent agents of euthanasia but they can induce respiratory distress in the patient. Generally, we prefer to employ concentrated solutions of pentobarbitone. This method has the advantage of being cheap, reliable, rapid and gentle. On the other hand, it has the inconvenience of requiring a vet's authority, these products being highly restricted on the market. Moreover, as the product remains in the animal's body, the cadavers are not suitable for processing within the agri-food industry but must be kept beyond the reach of scavengers and safely disposed of.

You're leaving the family home at last but you don't feel the relief you anticipated. Your metamorphosis has not yet happened. You are afraid.

For some animal liberation movements, the rights of all potential claimants should be granted without restriction. This should be extended to all living beings that cannot express themselves, including to animals, children, those with mental disabilities, the comatose and embryos. Animal rights militants are very often also anti-abortionists. For them, nature is always right.

You want to be like everyone else. You believe that being like everyone else makes people happy. You believe everyone is happy. You decide to get married. You instantly forget that, in *Cat People*, the wedding precedes the metamorphosis, and you're also forgetting that the metamorphosis heralds the heroine's unhappy ending.

I don't think I'd have been able to do experiments on cats or primates, luckily the question never came up, but I don't think I could've done it, except if I'd actually been forced to, I guess you can get used to anything and as I'm from a different generation I would surely have struggled to rebel, I'm the eldest in a large family, psychological tests show over and over that the older children are more obedient than the younger ones, I've always done what was expected of me, I've followed a completely classic path.

You are no eldest child but you have taken a very classic path. You're indifferent to your own desires, you neglect them, you ignore them. You watch Tourneur's *Cat People* with pleasure and alarm. Like everyone else who sees it, you're afraid of Irena Dubrovna, at least you say you are. You're afraid of her wildness, her metamorphosis, her needle-sharp claws, her cruelty. You're afraid because you're like everyone else, you need peace and quiet, you want to look alike to everyone, to have an orderly life, to build a home, to have children, to nurture a family, to make love on a regular basis with a regular partner whom everyone honours and respects. Yet at the end of the film, when the big cat has completed her transformation, when at last she is killed, when Mr Reed finds another, civilised, American woman, when order is re-established, when you ought to be congratulating yourself, you sink into your armchair and you weep, and weep on, you weep pointlessly, endlessly, blindly. You're still afraid. You're not reassured, not cured, not consoled. You are weeping.

IV

You like animals but that no longer matters at all. You have long been used to not having any, you can live with it, you can even see the advantages, you declare to whoever will listen that keeping a pet would destroy your freedom. This lets you put things in perspective or to ignore all the many other constraints you live with, though you don't know it.

Since childhood, I've always had animals in the house. My parents were country people. We raised farm animals, they stayed in the family, they weren't sold to outsiders, we slaughtered them regularly for our own consumption, it's natural to slaughter animals.

Despite your gestures of independence, you copy your elders, you repeat the behaviour of other members of your species since at least the first centuries of the Christian era. You've become an inadvertent enthusiast and practitioner of human ethology. You are well brought up and you're getting married.

We kept poultry, hens, chicks, we used to have them laying for twenty-one days, after that they fancied some action, you had to have a good cockerel, and then they'd have their chicks. Now that's all over, we buy our chicks already hatched, and we can't sell the eggs ourselves any more, for fear of spreading a disease, I don't remember the name of it but it's a disease you get from farm eggs, anyway if it means I have to get to market with my basket it's not worthwhile, I'd rather raise my own poultry for myself, you can't make a living off them but at least you can eat well.

You've heard that happiness has its price, you accept this, but despite your weak grasp of maths and economics you sometimes sense that the cost is higher than the benefit. You can't clearly distinguish what you owe from what you're owed, you're progressing in the dark, the contract binding you rules from on high and its precise terms remain obscure. You are struggling to extricate yourself, to understand yourself, to be your own person. You are well brought up.

Animal husbandry can be defined as the process of farming animals. The moment animals appear as an asset in your accounts, you've got a farm on your hands. This factor is necessary but not enough by itself; establishments where animals feature as stock (current assets) may fulfil the definition of a farm.

Being pig-ignorant about everything to do with accounting and legal language, I can't say if 'current assets' refers to animals running around in fields expressly set aside for them or to a column in the accounts that parallels and complements the column for liabilities.

Instead of going to the cinema with your mother, you now go with your husband. You hide your face in his chest when a film gets too violent and you look to him for comfort when they turn out very sad. You rewatch *King Kong*, *Dersu Uzala*, *The Wounded Man* and even *Rosemary's Baby*, which is a legendary and foundational film for you and of which you're now sure that you retain no pre-partum memory. You discuss characters, fear, compassion and identification with your husband. All your emotions are channelled by the art of cinema. You never mention the young man whom you loved as a teenager and who hanged himself in his bedroom. You are well brought up, you don't say a word.

In the interest of improving the quality of eggs inside the shell, whether liquid, frozen or dried, and to eliminate causes of discolouration, contamination or pollution during the various stages occurring outside the handling rooms, from collection to wholesaling, the dealers, reps, commissioners, tinning companies and makers of egg products must make use of facilities with the appropriate refrigeration apparatus and equipment for their respective activity.

Now, when you think about the reindeer, you picture a herd fleeing contaminated plains, grazing on irradiated grass alongside genetically modified hens and egg products of all kinds. You no longer believe in Father Christmas. Sometimes you miss him.

Generally when we kill a hen, it's because she's stopped laying, because after two or three years they're done, they don't lay any more or only very rarely. And my cock he's right over there, he's a very old cock, he's a good ten years old, a friend gave him to me, she only had three or four hens, poor things, what they only put up with, they didn't dare leave their roost in the morning because a cockerel normally likes to mount seven or eight hens and if there are only three, it can be a hard life for them.

You don't like your husband's desire, you don't like the frenzy of it, you don't like the transformation it triggers in him, you feel as if you're making love to someone else, you don't want to make love to anyone else, you'd prefer your husband to stay the same, you'd like to be reassured, protected, comforted; you're not frenzied, you're not carried away, you're not transformed. Your metamorphosis hasn't happened yet.

The study of human behaviour is substantially weighted towards studying domestic animals' behaviour. That said, industrial farming so drastically modifies the way animals live that it's impossible to apply observations made in high-yield cages or stables to any calm consideration of life in today's society.

You are living without jolts or clashes. You go on long journeys with your husband. You take the opportunity of travelling together in foreign lands to get closer to him. He is your refuge from the outside world. You sense your similarity. You're bonding with him. You encounter indigenous peoples with him. You concentrate on the sights before you. You're astonished, delighted, you're expanding your horizons. When you get back, nothing has changed. You still struggle to accept physical love-making and the transformations it creates. You don't want to move, you don't want to quiver, you don't want to reveal yourself. *Rosemary's Baby*, which you may have seen with your mother at the very beginning of your life, goes round and round in your head. Something about your life repels or horrifies you. You need reassurance. You're not ready yet.

There are four kinds of poultry farming: battery farming (code 3), in which each individual must have the use of 550 cm^2; floor-pen farming (code 2), in which the individual is kept inside but retains free movement; outdoor farming (code 1) in which the individual lives outside and has the use of a building for shelter in bad weather; and organic farming (code 0).

Contrary to our usual expectations of numbers, these codes are inversely proportionate to the supposed well-being of the animal. Rather, they appear directly proportionate to the profitability of the different kinds of farm. Besides, this classification has the advantage of enabling us to envisage future farms to be coded 4, 5 and above, whose practical features we currently struggle to imagine.

You avoid travelling around Siberia and Lake Baikal, afraid of seeing your childish daydreams confront a reality far removed from fairy tales. You know that reindeer now live on farms, that their numbers are known and tracked, that they have become used to temperate and humid regions, that they're no longer permitted to migrate to the East, that there are quotas for their slaughter, that their meat is prized and even that you could find yourself eating it one day.

Maman used to keep a sow. When it was time she'd bring it to the boar, then she'd wait for the births. Towards the end she had to watch the animal day and night because sows are huge, they sometimes crush their babies during birth. As my mother used to sell the piglets, she couldn't let them be crushed, she would keep two or three and sell the rest.

Work keeps you away from home several times a week. You stay in hotels some nights, winters follow winters, at no point do you consider telling the story of Father Christmas to any possible future children. You wonder if you're being haunted by the shadow of Rosemary, Polanski's protagonist. You tell your husband about your resistance. He agrees with you. You were well brought up, you still are.

We can teach pigs many things, they're very charming. If we tame them, they can come indoors, and there are people who keep pigs as pets. I find that a bit over the top because they get really fat, but they're so sweet, when we had to slaughter them it was dreadful, we couldn't bear having to give them up, we decided to stop keeping pigs altogether.

In the evenings when you're far from home, you dine with colleagues, you prepare your work for the following day, you speak to your husband on the phone, you don't take advantage of your repeated absences to take lovers, you think everything's fine. You've a notion that nothing will change in the shape of your life, and, instead of alarming you, this thought is a comfort. You speak to your husband about it. He agrees with you. You've been well brought up and you still are.

The facilities for housing the pigs must be built in such a way as to allow each pig to lie down, to rest and to stand up without difficulty, to have access to a clean area in which to rest and to be able to see other pigs.

You move easily into professional life. You begin to see what it is you are aiming for. You're afraid of getting stuck here but equally afraid of making a change. You feel trapped. You talk to your husband about it, he agrees with you. And as you're well brought up, you go on.

When the pigs are tied up, their rope must not hurt them and must be inspected on a regular basis and adjusted whenever necessary so that they're happy. Each rope must be long enough to allow the animals to move around. They must be tied in such a way as to avoid, as far as possible, all risk of strangulation and injury.

Your surroundings weigh on you. One day, heading off with friends to be far from family and your husband, you start to realise what you miss and what attracts you.

You return more downcast, more alone and more fragile but also far surer of yourself.

If pigs are kept together, measures must be taken to avoid scuffles that go beyond everyday behaviour. Pigs showing ongoing hostility towards other pigs and the victims of this aggression must be separated or distanced from the group.

During your trips away with work, you meet a woman ten years younger than you. In the beginning you see her every now and then but, as time passes, though unplanned, your encounters become customary, regular, weekly. At first, you don't think about it, you have no expectations, the young woman shows up every week, you have a coffee in town with her, you chat, you go to bed without necessarily having called your husband. You've been well brought up. You'll stay that way.

The boars' enclosures must be built so that they can turn around and take in the grunts, smells and shapes of the other pigs. As for the pregnant sows, they must be moved into farrowing pens where the dimensions must be sufficient for their piglets to suckle without difficulty.

On one of your trips, when it's been several months of your weekly coffees with this woman ten years younger, she doesn't come. You find that her absence leaves a gap. You wait for her. All that week, you think about her. You say nothing to your husband so as not to worry him. In order to lie, you'd have to speak. You're well brought up, you mean to stay that way.

Pigs must not be kept in constant darkness. With this in mind, and to fulfil their behavioural and physiological needs, suitable natural or artificial lighting may be provided; for the latter, this must be at least equivalent to the period of natural light normally available between 9 a.m. and 5 p.m. Additionally, a suitable fixed or mobile light of sufficient intensity to enable inspection of the pigs at any time must also be available.

When you return for work the following week, you're afraid that the woman ten years younger than you whom you've got used to seeing on every trip may not be there. That day, you're especially happy to see her. You don't tell her so, nor that her absence has been more difficult than you expected. Silence is another kind of lie. You were well brought up. You still are.

All the pigs must be fed at least once a day. When pigs are housed in groups and don't have access to food as and when they wish or to any automatic feeding system, each pig must be given access to food at the same time as all the other animals in the group.

You stay away from home a little longer than usual to join a few work meetings that previously you'd have had no qualms about missing. You talk to your husband about this, he agrees with you. The coffees you have with the woman ten years younger turn into dinners.

In order to avoid caudophagia, that is, the chewing or biting off of fellow pigs' tails, a 'painful form of anomalous behaviour observed under conditions of intensive breeding', as it's described by the European Food Safety Authority, caudectomy is widely practised. Carried out shortly after a piglet's birth, this consists of cutting off the animal's tail. In the pork industry, this operation is part of what we call 'piglet care'.

The most reliable way to remedy the suffering which prompts an individual to attack its fellow consists not in eradicating the cause of hostility but in eradicating all or part of the fellow creature.

As far as possible, you avoid encounters with colleagues in your office or outside it. You don't wish them to know why you systematically decline their invitations. You continue to dine regularly with the woman who's ten years younger. You are well brought up, you are learning to live in hiding.

When the pig began to squeal I used to run away, we were living in a village, so when I heard it I'd hotfoot it straight to school which was just behind the house. That's how I learnt to read and write, thanks to the pig, it squealed, it was vast, I went to school to get away from the pig's squeals.

With the woman who's ten years younger you go to restaurants where you're unlikely to bump into your colleagues. When you happen to encounter one, you greet them distractedly. You're well brought up, you mean to stay that way.

To allow them to satisfy their behavioural needs, all the pigs – with due consideration for their environment and population density – must have access to straw. The absence of straw, or of some other substratum enabling rooting, and the presence of slatted floors and a bare environment will, on the other hand, promote aggressive behaviour between individuals. The provision of toys such as ropes, chewy sticks and balls, despite not substantially reducing the risks of caudophagia, may calm the animals and diminish general violence between fellow pigs.

Your meetings with the woman ten years younger have become essential to your personal equilibrium. You say nothing about this to your husband. You'd have to say something in order to lie. You think you've done nothing wrong but you also think you may soon leave the city or go into hiding. You are preparing.

On those mornings we had to get up very early and put water on to boil in a great cast-iron pot, we'd go back into the courtyard, catch one by the trotter, four or five of us holding it down, we'd carry it outside, I don't think that hurt but they'd be afraid, more than anything, that's why they used to squeal, I never watched but I know how it used to go, one of them would stick the knife in, that was his job, I mean he was a farmer like the rest but at this time of year he was the one who did that job and he made a fair packet out of it, if he could fit three or four in a morning. After that we'd scald it and scrape it to get all the hair off, that was the men's job. The women would generally be busy stirring the blood from the bloodletting that we'd gathered in a basin, you had to keep it runny and stop lumps forming, then, when the carcass had been split in two, they'd wash the guts out several times over while the men went off to play cards. We didn't like killing the pig at all but that didn't kill our appetites, we were all set up with excellent-quality cold cuts for the rest of the year.

You don't like spending time at the office and you don't like the countryside, either. On the other hand, you can hardly wait for your dinners with the young woman ten years your junior. You don't mention them to your husband. In order to lie, you'd have to speak. You are preparing.

Pigs make for a lot of work all year round, what's more they can fall ill, they get fevers, they come out in red splotches, it's a kind of measles, sometimes they even die of it although most of them won't, they decline slowly until they give up the ghost, that happened to us once or twice, it's a real blow to the pocket as we don't eat dead animals, if they die by themselves they can't be eaten.

One evening when you've drunk too much, you sit plumb on the ground in the middle of town with the younger woman, you talk until late into the night, you describe your suffocating relationship with your mother, you talk about the grief you've been carrying with you, you discover that you're angry with the whole world, your anger is on the verge of being expressed. Returning to your hotel in the early hours, you decide that you're too old for such outpourings, that people could have seen you, at the same time you wonder why you're feeling so feather-light. You're on the point of letting yourself go.

Transferring the pigs from the unloading platform to the stockyards should be a simple process and should not require protracted staff intervention. The storage bays should be clearly identified so that the pig keeper understands the order in which the animals should be moved. The pigs themselves must be able to move smoothly towards the trap where they will be stunned and then bled.

One day you are feverish, you don't go away for work, you pace back and forth like a trapped tiger, you feel hot, you feel cold, you feel locked in, you'd like to let the woman ten years younger know, you don't have her number and even if you had it, a call from you might appear presumptuous. You brood.

In the corridors known as feeder corridors or death rows, facilities must be provided that give the animals no way of turning back or escaping. The corridors must therefore be narrow yet without constraining regular additions to the line. Every incident, jostling or traffic jam, every animal that trips with concomitant cries and panicked movements, can in practice lead to a temporary halt in the production line and proportionately reduce the yield.

With the woman who's ten years younger, you talk about the young man whom you loved and who hanged himself in his bedroom. A tide of emotion overwhelms you, you begin to cry. You discover that losing your self-control offers unexpected pleasures. You are preparing.

The layout of the trap and the anaesthesia zone must also be planned such that staff may operate with ease without coming into direct contact with the animals. Restraining equipment must, in addition, be provided for cases of ineffective anaesthesia; as far as possible, all animals should be immobilised before they lose consciousness, both to protect staff from potential injury and to allow them easily to locate where on the pre-anaesthetised animal to target for the greatest impact on brain function.

It's been a long time since you stopped believing in fairy tales but your ideas about love are still very naïve. You're trying to protect yourself. You're trying to distance yourself. You're keeping yourself and the truth apart. You're trying to be numb, to tranquillise yourself, to dull your mind. You feel guilty, you're angry with the woman ten years younger, you disparage what makes you happy. You don't say a word to your husband. To lie, you'd have to talk. You brood.

The piercing stunner, the spring-loaded stunner and electrocution clamps are the three most common weapons used to stun animals before they're bled. Loss of consciousness is a requirement. It causes the animal immediate loss of balance and respiratory arrest as well as tonic cramps (deep, protracted muscle contractions). It is recommended that bleeding be carried out within the minute following loss of consciousness. In fact, studies have shown that meat quality is inversely proportionate to the animal's stress levels directly before death.

You try to control your emotions, to anaesthetise your senses, to suppress your outbursts, to distance yourself from the woman who's ten years younger than you, to avoid her, detach yourself, to attain that old, familiar somnambulist state, to be numb, distracted, dulled, blind as you were before. You instate a regulation distance between you and her, you keep to it, you focus, during the periods you spend on work trips you stay head down, you don't answer your phone, you eat at the hotel, you drink whisky, you get drunk, you watch the TV screwed to the ceiling, you turn off the sound, you channel-hop, you get dizzy, dull, you fill your head, you drain yourself. You lock your door as though someone might try to force it, you barricade yourself in as though someone were threatening you, you keep close to the walls as if someone were spying on you, you speak softly as if someone were listening. But when you realise that no one is spying, or listening, or pursuing or hassling or threatening you, or trying to force your door, you sink into melancholy. You are riven with doubt, weird and unlikely images crowd your dreams, you try to push them away, strange voices whisper in your ears, you pretend not to hear them. Your efforts come to nothing. You're afraid of giving way, succumbing, screaming, desiring. You're on the point of metamorphosing.

One evening just before Christmas, you dine with the woman ten years younger than you, and snow starts to fall. Instead of going back to your hotel, you end up in her bed and you make love. Silence envelops you. Silence surrounds you. Silence enfolds you. You fall silent. You hide. Through fear, politeness, impotence, shame, weakness, you go into hiding.

I've no wish to know what happens to my cows after I sell them, they go to Italy, it's a network, they'll either keep them or sell them on to people, I don't know what they do and I don't care.

In the morning you go to work, you think about the night before as an experience without consequences, a knot in the straightforward course of your life, a swerve. You don't consider what you'll do after Christmas. You're well brought up, you desire above all to stay that way. You're lying to yourself.

True, it's always a bit strange taking animals to the abattoir that you've bred, cared for, groomed and petted, but there's nothing special about killing them, that's nature, you just have to not think about it too much.

The woman ten years younger calls several times in the morning, you try to persuade yourself of the insignificance of the night's events, you fake indifference to reassure yourself but you can't help seeing her again that day. You miss the train you'd planned to catch. You realise that things are not going to be as simple as you expected. You consider without articulating it what you'll do after Christmas. You're on the verge of setting yourself free.

It happened in the field behind the house. The livestock dealer got here, we told him, that bull you sold us, we're not too sure, he's jumpy, he's a big scrawny bugger, he's nervous and we're a bit worried. The dealer went into the field, I can still see him with his cane, the bull charged him, then stopped a couple of metres short. Then, instead of backing out, he made a professional error. With that club of his he walloped the bull as hard as he could, he gave him great whacks round the head to show him who was boss. The bull got angry, he attacked him head-on and wouldn't let go. We saw what was happening and got in there like lightning, we managed to get the bull to back off using the tractor but the dealer was smashed to a pulp, he didn't die on the spot, he had internal haemorrhaging, poor sod. As for the bull, he went straight to the abattoir, I don't even know if they paid us.

Although you no longer believe in Father Christmas, you'd like to run away with the reindeer, see Lake Baikal, take a route towards the Urals, all the way to the Chinese border. You are tempted by this flight with the herd but you don't feel strong enough to do it alone, alone is something you've never been. You propose to your husband that he come too. He says yes. You don't want to be set free quite yet.

Generally, when they go to the abattoir it all flows smoothly, even if we get the odd tricksy one, we have to corner them in the corridors as best we can, turn them the right way, push them, so they'll walk up by themselves without needing any shots. It's a complete system: it's our job to set them up so they go in by themselves. Also, it's better to avoid the lasso because, not being used to ropes and such, they fight it when you try to tie them and that's when they can get dangerous.

You ask your husband to let you spend a day with the woman who's ten years younger, you promise him that you need to go so you can break up with her. He lets you go. You go for a spontaneous day-return, you explain to her that you'll never leave your husband, she cries, you're upset by her tears, you explain that it's all too sudden, she's still crying, you can't think what to say or do. You stay in bed with her the whole day and when you catch the train back, you realise that you've resolved nothing. You would like to spend the Christmas holidays with her.

This year, I brought a cow to the abattoir and she got out of her pen, she tried to hurdle it, stuck her horns in the bars and tore them away, then she got out of the abattoir's grounds, and after that there was no catching her. She charged us, then went off towards the town. We had to call the police in and a vet with a hypodermic gun to take out our cow, wait for her to drop off, borrow a tractor that was passing that way, take her back to the abattoir, give her an injection to wake her up before we could kill her, we couldn't kill her while she was asleep because she first had to get the anaesthetic out of her system. She went completely nuts but that's very rare, usually it always goes fine.

You and your husband go sledging and to see reindeer. You visit a farm, you are shown the opencast mines and natural gas terminals around the animals' pastures. You take a snow bike with the farmer, bringing fodder to deer that, due to industrial encroachment into their former grazing grounds, are no longer surviving on what they can forage. You watch them ruminate and ruminate. Now you know what the reindeer do after Christmas. Disenchantment is just one more route to intellectual emancipation.

The cow, of course not, she has no idea she's going to die. She goes dumbly on into the abattoir just as she'd walk into a field, she knows it's a bad place for her, of course, if she could choose I can tell you she'd do an about-turn just like that, but she can't. No. She doesn't know she's going to die. She knows she's not in her natural environment, she's trapped, something's going to happen, anyway, no matter which animal you back into a corner, they know they're in danger. And there are very particular sounds there, smells that tell her it's dangerous, but they don't think like we do, animals, they don't know they're going to die. She couldn't possibly know.

You let the cold, the snow and the sledging fill your mind. You're trying to forget the woman ten years younger than you. You're trying to hold back the impulses that course through you. You're practising self-control, self-mastery. You think of the cat woman, you don't want to end up like her. Death does not seem a good solution. You're looking for another but finding nothing. You're delaying your emancipation.

The animals are always well treated, the professionals look after them well. Of course, if you order over a batch of cows from Poland to be slaughtered in Toulouse, a few will take a tumble inside the lorry and the others will trample over them, that happens, but they're wrong to do it like that, that's all, you won't find a guy like me going about it that way, people talk a lot of crap but all in all, there's never any real problems, the animals are always well treated.

All your effort adds up to nothing. The change of scene makes no difference. You don't want to die. You don't believe the fairy tales they told you as a child. You're not like the cat woman. You don't live in America. You aren't married to an American. You've no intention of refusing to sleep with your husband for fear of what might happen. You don't wish to change from victim to predator, nor from predator to victim. You are neither dominated, nor dominatrix. You are luckier than the cat woman. You have more freedom to act than the cat woman. You have greater desire than the cat woman. You are stronger than her. You weren't born before the war. Your parents weren't Serbian. They haven't left you alone in a foreign country. You are no panther. You're not metamorphosing into an animal. You stop identifying with her. You stop holding back. You stop reining yourself in. You accept the impulses moving through you. You're surprised, you're determined, and combative, you're a rebel, you're untamed, you are joyful, you are light. Your parents' betrayal is imminent. You are ready.

When you get back, the woman ten years younger asks you to leave your husband or to end it with her. You try to avoid doing either one or the other, to make both pleasure and pain go on. You're disgusted by your own indecision but you dig your heels in.

I wanted to be a butcher because I wanted to kill things. Maybe it frightened me at first but I also liked the idea, I wanted to be a butcher so I could kill animals.

Although you're sure the few nights you spent with the young woman were senseless, you want more. More nights. You are flooded by a wave of naïve love, you're carried away, emotion is making you stupid. The young woman hits back over your indecision: you may only visit when she decides, you bend to her will, to her desire, she makes you wait, this time yes, another time no, you're behaving like a teenager, you can't seem to get away. You're hungry for her flesh, her smell, you want to drink her, smell her, suck her, bite her, your desire is wild, you're beside yourself, you tremble, you scream, you're transforming, you're exposed. You're metamorphosing.

I begged my parents to let me be a butcher but they wanted me to go to school. One day, I was eleven, someone had a pig to slaughter, my dad told me, you want to be a butcher, just kill that pig. There were four or five of them to catch it and the one who'd usually kill it showed me where to aim with the knife, and it went really well, it bled, a perfect job. Then, as I hadn't chickened out, my parents found someone to take me on and I did what I always wanted, I became a butcher.

Unlike the cat woman, your metamorphosis does not herald the end of you. Emancipation takes forms you never imagined.

Calves are just like pigs only easier, because you can cut their throats right across. With calves you'll end up cutting their heads off anyway without having to try too hard, whereas with pigs you have to be quite precise, the pig has to stay whole. But in general, whichever animal it is, you just have to cut through the artery in the neck, it's always the same action.

When at last you decide to leave your husband, it's too late to think of any kind of relationship with the young woman. For some time now, you've wished you'd done things differently, you even hope it might be possible for you to go back, to pick up conjugal life where you left it. You're afraid your separation could hand the reins back to your parents; you do not wish to go back to the cinema with your mother. At the same time, you're learning to live by yourself, you're detaching, extracting yourself, you're listening to your feelings, you're no longer sleepwalking, numb, dazed, distracted, dulled, blind, withdrawn. You're often sad, you weep, you think about the young man you loved who hanged himself in his room, you're recalling yourself, you're talking, you're trying to be your own woman. You are reaching for freedom.

As a kid I thought it was cool to kill animals, I was impressed by the boys who did it, I thought it took guts and I admired them, though it's easy really, you just need to be strong, stick a knife into flesh, there's nothing special in that.

You fall in love with a woman who doesn't know exactly what she wants. You don't, either. You stray together and separately, you wonder what your future holds and even if you'll have one. After a few months, she leaves you, starts seeing a man, buys an apartment, has two children and creates a family life which looks less attractive to you by the second. You are miserable when she leaves, you realise that you need to abandon the ideas you had as a little girl of how your grown-up life would be. To free yourself, you first have to give things up.

We had a C-section, the first time I've seen that, it was awful. We'd tied the cow by her horns and then we started feeling inside her, we realised the calf was the wrong way round. The vet came, he put his hand inside, he said, she needs a C-section, go get a table, a sheet, soap and hot water. He started injecting her, he shaved her, made an incision, it was horrendous, he took out everything that was inside and put it on the table, you see that living thing there on the table, I can't explain, it was a horror show, the calf itself was dead, it was too much for it, the vet had to take out the placenta, then put the whole womb back inside, sew it all up double quick, it took all afternoon, cost us a fortune and the cow was screwed, next calving she won't make it, so we're forced to get rid of her.

You give up on toeing the line, pleasing your parents, bearing children, telling fairy tales, going into raptures over motherhood. You know now how to betray them. And that's what you're doing. You're betraying them.

I started out in abattoirs and I did all the jobs there. I can describe them if you like. In the dirty zone there's the stunning, the hooking up, there's the bleeding, there's what we call the 'snout and horns', we peel the snout off the face, there's the hide removal: first trotter, second trotter, and then we cut off the front trotters, skin the head, back feet, truss up at the back, we put a knot in the digestive tract where it passes close to the larynx so it doesn't chuck grass all round our animal's insides, then there's the evisceration, and the skin comes off. Next we move to the clean zone, open the sternum, cleave the chest in two, take off the head, then out comes the white offal, the small and large intestines, and the dark offal, the liver and lights, they go to the vets, and after that the fat goes for rendering, deboning fore and hind, chopping it up and finishing, then weighing and classing. I don't have a favourite job, I like them all.

You watch *Silent Light*, a film by Carlos Reygadas, without your mother. The main character lives through a great love story with a woman who isn't his wife. At the end of the film, the wife dies. The main character weeps. The woman he loves comes to see him on the day of the funeral and tells him: we can't go back to how we were. For the first time, this certainty does not plunge you into depression. You even feel a kind of satisfaction weighing the consequences of this phenomenon. You say the line to yourself over and over. We can't go back to how we were. It enters and permeates you. Thanks to the art of cinema, you accept this idea, you feel better for it, you even think it's good news. You're freeing yourself.

The production line is an industrial thing. The living and dead circuits never cross and it can't ever change direction, it goes forward. We get through 400 animals a day, we're sixty on the line, that makes fifty-eight animals per hour and it's all without violence, if the first shot doesn't do the job, we give them a second one, the animals don't suffer. We could of course kill more per hour but then they pile up down the line, we have to wait for them to get going again, it's not the killing that takes the time, it's everything else.

Your relationship with your ex-husband is a continuation of your relationship with your mother. You decide to divorce him. You know at last how to betray them, and you're thrilled. When the day comes, you wait to go before the judge, a name is called, no one replies, you realise after a few minutes that this name is your married name and it's you they're calling.

This issue of traceability is pointless. They mark where the cattle come from. That doesn't get us anywhere. The food the cow eats, whether from the piggery here or in Belgium, makes no difference. They've fixed us up to sell it. Telling people that French meat is the best was all about fudging the issue. What we feed them has nothing to do with the animal's origins, it's totally dumb. The whole point is it sucks up to the supermarkets. It does nothing for us and if they go on with their bloody rules and regs, we'll soon go out of business.

After your divorce, some people persist in calling you by your married name, which, in any case, you never used yourself. The whole thing annoys you.

At your age, you'll have to think about having kids now otherwise it will be too late. You don't want children. You don't want to be a mother. Everything annoys you.

Despite your explanations, your gynaecologist doesn't really understand that your sexuality has changed. Still no sexual relationship? he continues to ask in a troubled voice at every appointment. Everything annoys you.

You write a script about a love story between two women. The producer suggests you keep the same plot, only change the sex of one of the protagonists, it won't be so different between a man and a woman and it'll be more universal. Everything annoys you.

Some of your friends who've become parents aren't happy to leave their three-year-old daughter with you because you never know, it could give the little one wrong ideas. Everything annoys you.

Work contacts who call you at home tangle themselves in apologies when they hear another woman's voice on the line. Everything annoys you.

You are forty-four years old and still people call you 'mademoiselle'. Everything annoys you.

When you walk hand in hand with a woman in the streets of an average town, pedestrians stare at you and turn to watch you go by. Everything annoys you.

We understand, we support you, it can't be easy, homosexuality is a real problem. Everything annoys you.

You are astonished, you're disarmed, you control nothing, keep track of nothing, you're inspired, annoyed, involved, impatient. After decades of holding back, of restraint and self-denial, you no longer have time for self-justification or patience. You release what you've had pent up for so many years, you express yourself.

You discover rage. It surges in you. It accompanies you. It supports you. It helps. You rely on it. It keeps you alive and aware.

In my butcher's shop, I've no beef with anyone. Select my cow. Bring it out. Chop it up. Give it to the customer. The customer comes back and tells me how tasty it was. And my passion is for live purchase. I buy the cow still on its feet, and then the pleasure of choosing an excellent product, I get to set that out on display just as it was in the field, that's what I enjoy most in my job.

You're not unhappy to find out and the information even has the benefit of reassuring you. There is as much satisfaction in recognising death in the living as in seeing life in the dead.

No one likes the killers at the abattoir, people think it's nasty work, especially when they're allocated the dirty zone. When I see the young kids who come here, sometimes they stay half a day then turn round and go home, it's physical labour, to kill you need to be a man.

You're not unhappy to discover this and, what's more, the information cheers you up. At the abattoir, it isn't women who deal in death, it's the men.

Meat from heifers is younger, so it's tenderer. When the cows have a calf, they get thinner along the back, they lose muscle mass, everything that goes into the rib-eye and the sirloin is thinner, less juicy. They'll be eaten just the same except if we're being fussy about yield and quality, we're better off with animals that haven't calved.

You're not unhappy to learn it and the information even has the power to make you smile. Animals that haven't calved taste better than the rest.

I choose three-and-a-half-year-old cows, otherwise they're not mature enough, not sufficiently grown-up. And I only buy females, I don't go for the males because the meat tends to be tougher. The females are more tender, fattier and better shaped, their finest cuts are bigger.

You're not unhappy to learn it and the information even has the power to delight you. Females taste better than males.

There are cuts that we sell fresh and others which must first be hung. The outer cuts lose their colour very quickly, the sirloin, the shank have to be sold within six days, otherwise they dry out. Whereas the rib and the roasting joint can be kept almost three weeks. Except if you cut into the meat to take a slice, then you have to sell it quickly otherwise it'll go off. As long as you keep it in its fat and with the nerves intact, the meat will mature, but you have to keep an eye on it because there's a point when it starts to turn and a point when it's rotting.

You're not unhappy to learn this and the information even has the power to comfort you. There's a big difference between maturity and going rotten.

My own approach, well, it's just the way I like to do it, I'm not saying it's the best way. But what I like is animals brought up almost exclusively on grass. I avoid animals brought up on pellets in their stalls, I don't go for that. The one I'll kill for Christmas, the farmer's keeping her for me, she's a real beauty, I'll take you to see her.

He's going to take you to see her. He's going to show you the animal he'll be killing for Christmas.

For good local veal, your calf absolutely can't have been running around with its mother in the fields otherwise it'll have been drinking milk and eating grass. If you're after white meat, not red, the calf has to get a little anaemic, it has to stay indoors and have no opportunity to ruminate.

You're not unhappy to learn it and the information even has the power to astonish you. Good meat doesn't necessarily come from an animal running freely in the fields and living in constant contact with its mother. You are losing a little of your naïvety.

The van comes twice a week and brings them to me quartered, otherwise I'd never be able to carry them inside. I take them to the abattoir on Mondays, they're back with me by the Thursday. Once they're in the fridge, I can sell the tongue, the tail, the outer meat right away, I have to wait for the rest, I've to wait five days before getting to that. It has to settle.

You're not unhappy to learn it and the information even has the power to encourage you. To be edible, you have to be relaxed.

In the twenty years I've been doing this job, it's only happened once that a client has said I'm not coming next week because it's my cow you have there and I won't eat that meat. Usually the farmers who buy their meat from me love to see their own cow in my window, they're especially happy about it that week and they buy more to keep in the freezer.

You're not unhappy to learn this and the information even has the power to strengthen you. We eat with greater pleasure and better appetite the creatures that we love.

Your encounter with the butcher changes your ideas about fairy tales and cannibalism. You think again of the animal corpses that you never held in your hands, of the young man hanged in his bedroom, of those you didn't know how to love. You unlock your doors, you open your gates, you weep less over *Cat People* and more over your own memories. You are awakening.

You choose to return to your own body and set up your home there. You choose to betray your mother so as not to betray yourself. You are awakening.

You allow images of the past to forge paths into your mind. You let emotion overtake you. You no longer need to be recognised and admired and well-adapted and assimilated and integrated. You are betraying society without a single backward glance. You are awakening.

You think again of all those films that you saw with your mother, and of the way you'll watch them again now, of those you've seen since, of the connections you'll now maintain with sex, violence and death, of your education in pleasure, in anger, in sadness and in tears, of necessary separations and what they leave behind. You're no longer afraid, you're no longer ashamed, you no longer belong to your mother, nor to your husband, you are living your wild life while still being civilised, you speak, you shiver, you sniff, you lick, you bite, you stroke, you eat meat, you listen to butchers, you're not disgusted, you're not nauseated, you laugh, you criticise, you sympathise, you love, you stay aware, you're neither protected nor disarmed, nor imprinted, you don't mourn your childhood, the golden age, the very beginning, the so-called innocence, you don't stand against the rest of the world, silence is not your weapon of choice, you accept the idea that reindeer are transported in refrigerated lorries, you don't believe in Father Christmas, you don't follow the sledge, age has set you free.

My most heartfelt thanks go first to David Moinard and to Stéphane Thidet who, in 2009, asked me to write a text for *Estuaire*, an intervention organised by the Lieu Unique arts centre in Nantes, which text formed the basis for this book.

Thanks too to Catherine Tambrun, Francky Lestrade, Gérard Dousseau, Georges Chapouthier, François Lachapelle, Annette, Francis, Patrick and Marie-Line Pesquidoux, Georges Jarry, Fabrice Requier, Rudy Wierdlarski, Dominique Parot-Lafon, Catherine Remy, Fabien Jobard, Philippe Bretelle, Laurent Larivière, Béatrice Mousli-Bennett, Yves Pagès and Nicole Combezou, without whom this book could never have happened.

Dear readers,

As well as relying on bookshop sales, And Other Stories relies on subscriptions from people like you for many of our books, whose stories other publishers often consider too risky to take on.

Our subscribers don't just make the books physically happen. They also help us approach booksellers, because we can demonstrate that our books already have readers and fans. And they give us the security to publish in line with our values, which are collaborative, imaginative and 'shamelessly literary'.

All of our subscribers:

- receive a first-edition copy of each of the books they subscribe to
- are thanked by name at the end of our subscriber-supported books
- receive little extras from us by way of thank you, for example: postcards created by our authors

BECOME A SUBSCRIBER, OR GIVE A SUBSCRIPTION TO A FRIEND

Visit andotherstories.org/subscriptions to help make our books happen. You can subscribe to books we're in the process of making. To purchase books we have already published, we urge you to support your local or favourite bookshop and order directly from them – the often unsung heroes of publishing.

OTHER WAYS TO GET INVOLVED

If you'd like to know about upcoming events and reading groups (our foreign-language reading groups help us choose books to publish, for example) you can:

- join our mailing list at: andotherstories.org
- follow us on Twitter: @andothertweets
- join us on Facebook: facebook.com/AndOtherStoriesBooks
- admire our books on Instagram: @andotherpics
- follow our blog: andotherstories.org/ampersand

This book was made possible thanks to the support of:

Aaron McEnery · Aaron Schneider · Abby Shackelford · Abigail Charlesworth · Adam Bowman · Adam Lenson · Adelle Stripe · Aileen-Elizabeth Taylor · Ailsa Peate · Aisling Reina · Ajay Sharma · Alan McMonagle · Alan Simpson · Alasdair Hutchison · Alastair Gillespie · Alastair Laing · Alex Fleming · Alex Hancock · Alex Ramsey · Alexander Bunin · Alexandra Citron · Alexandra de Verseg-Roesch · Alexandra Stewart · Alexandra Stewart · Alfred Birnbaum · Ali Casey · Ali Conway · Ali Smith · Alice Clarke · Alicia Bishop · Alison Lock · Alison Riley · Alison Winston · Alistair McNeil · Aliya Rashid · Alyse Ceirante · Alyssa Tauber · Amado Floresca · Amanda · Amanda Silvester · Amber Da · Amelia Ashton · Amelia Dowe · Amine Hamadache · Amitav Hajra · Amy Benson · Amy Bojang · Ana Savitzky · Anastasia Carver · Andrea Reece · Andrew Kerr-Jarrett · Andrew Marston · Andrew McCallum · Andrew Rego · Andrew Wilkinson · Aneesa Higgins · Angela Everitt · Angharad Jones · Ann Moore · Ann Sheasby · Anna Glendenning · Anna Milsom · Anna Pigott · Anna-Maria Aurich · Anne Carus · Anne Frost · Anne Goldsmith ·

Anne Guest · Anne Ryden · Anne Stokes · Anne-Marie Renshaw · Anneliese O'Malley · Annie McDermott · Anonymous · Anonymous · Anthony Quinn · Antonia Lloyd-Jones · Antonio de Swift · Antony Pearce · Aoife Boyd · Archie Davies · Arne Van Petegem · Asako Serizawa · Asher Norris · Audrey Mash · Avril Marren · Barbara Mellor · Barbara Wheatley · Barry John Fletcher · Ben Schofield · Ben Thornton · Ben Walter · Benjamin Judge · Bettina Rogerson · Beverly Jackson · Bianca Jackson · Bianca Winter · Bill Fletcher · Brandon Knibbs · Brendan McIntyre · Briallen Hopper · Brian Anderson · Brian Byrne · Bridget Gill · Bridget McGeechan · Brigita Ptackova · Burkhard Fehsenfeld · Caitlin Halpern · Caitlin Liebenberg · Caitriona Lally · Callie Steven · Cameron Lindo · Caren Harple · Carl Emery · Carla Carpenter · Carlos Gonzalez · Carol Christie · Carol McKay · Carolina Pineiro · Caroline Bennett · Caroline Haufe · Caroline Lodge · Caroline Mager · Caroline Maldonado · Caroline Picard · Caroline Smith · Caroline Waight · Caroline West · Carolyn Johnson · Cassidy

Hughes · Catharine Braithwaite · Catharine Mee · Catherine Bailey · Catherine Lambert · Catherine Rodden · Catherine Thomas · Cathy Czauderna · Catie Kosinski · Catriona Gibbs · Cecilia Rossi · Cecilia Uribe · Cecily Maude · Chantal Wright · Charles Fernyhough · Charles Raby · Charles Wolfe · Charles Dee Mitchell · Charlotte Briggs · Charlotte Holtam · Charlotte Murrie & Stephen Charles · Charlotte Ryland · Charlotte Whittle · Chia Foon Yeow · China Miéville · Chris Gostick · Chris Gribble · Chris Lintott · Chris Maguire · Chris McCann · Chris Stevenson · Chris Young · Chris & Kathleen Repper-Day · Christian Kopf · Christine Bartels · Christine Dyer · Christine Phillips · Christopher Allen · Christopher Stout · Christopher Whiffin · Ciara Ní Riain · Claire Ashman · Claire Malcolm · Claire Riley · Claire Tristram · Claire Williams · Clare Archibald · Clari Marrow · Clarice Borges · Claudia Nannini · Claudio Scotti · Cliona Quigley · Clive Bellingham · Colin Denyer · Colin Matthews · Courtney Lilly · Cyrus Massoudi · Dag Bennett · Dale Wisely · Dan Raphael · Daniel Arnold · Daniel

Coxon · Daniel
Gallimore · Daniel
Gillespie · Daniel Hahn ·
Daniel Sweeney · Daniel
Venn · Daniel Wood ·
Daniela Steierberg ·
Darcy Hurford · Darina
Brejtrova · Darius
Cuplinskas · Dave
Lander · Davi Rocha ·
David Anderson · David
Hebblethwaite · David
Higgins · David Irvine ·
David Johnson-Davies ·
David Mantero · David
McIntyre · David Miller ·
David Shriver · David
Smith · David Steege ·
David Travis · David F
Long · Dean Taucher ·
Debbie Pinfold · Declan
Gardner · Declan
O'Driscoll · Deirdre Nic
Mhathuna · Delaina
Haslam · Denis Larose ·
Denis Stillewagt & Anca
Fronescu · Diana Cragg ·
Diana Digges · Dominic
Nolan · Dominick Santa
Cattarina · Duncan
Clubb · Duncan Marks ·
Dylan Tripp · E
Rodgers · Eamon Flack ·
Ed Burness · Ed Owles ·
Ed Tronick · Eimear
McNamara · Ekaterina
Beliakova · Eleanor
Dawson · Eleanor
Maier · Elena Tincu-
Straton · Elie Howe ·
Elina Zicmane ·
Elisabeth Cook · Eliza
O'Toole · Elizabeth
Cochrane · Elizabeth
Draper · Elizabeth
Franz · Elizabeth Leach ·
Elizabeth Soydas · Ellen
Wilkinson · Ellie
Goddard · Elliot
Marcus · Elvira
Kreston-Brody · Emily
Bromfield · Emily
Taylor · Emily
Williams · Emily
Yaewon Lee & Gregory
Limpens · Emily

Webber · Emma
Bielecki · Emma Knock ·
Emma Musty · Emma
Page · Emma Parker ·
Emma Perry · Emma
Post · Emma Reynolds ·
Emma Teale · Emma
Turesson · Emma Louise
Grove · Erin Cameron
Allen · Erin Louttit ·
Ewan Tant · F Gary
Knapp · Fatima Kried ·
Fawzia Kane · Filiz
Emre-Cooke · Finbarr
Farragher · Fiona Davis ·
Fiona Liddle · Fiona
Quinn · Florence
Reynolds · Florian
Duijsens · Fran
Sanderson · Frances de
Pontes Peebles · Francis
Mathias · Frank van
Orsouw · Friederike
Knabe · Gabriel Vogt ·
Gabriela Lucia Garza de
Linde · Gabrielle
Crockatt · Garan
Holcombe · Gary
Gorton · Gavin Collins ·
Gavin Smith · Gawain
Espley · Genaro Palomo
Jr · Geoff Fisher · Geoff
Thrower · Geoffrey
Cohen · Geoffrey
Urland · George
Christie · George
Hawthorne · George
McCaig · George
Stanbury · George
Wilkinson · Georgia
Panteli · Geraldine
Brodie · German
Cortez-Hernandez ·
Gerry Craddock · Gill
Adey · Gill Boag-
Munroe · Gill Osborne ·
Gillian Grant · Gillian
Spencer · Glen Bornais ·
Gordon Cameron ·
Graham Fulcher ·
Graham R Foster ·
Gregory Ford · Guy
Haslam · Gwyn Lewis ·
Hadil Balzan · Hamish
Russell · Hank Pryor ·
Hannah Dougherty ·

Hannah Harford-
Wright · Hannah
Procter · Hannah Jane
Lownsbrough · Hans
Lazda · Harriet Stiles ·
Heather Tipon · Helen
Brady · Helen Collins ·
Helen Coombes · Helen
Waland · Helen
Wormald · Henrike
Laehnemann · Henry
Patino · Hilary
McGrath · Holly Pester ·
Howard Robinson ·
Hugh Gilmore ·
Hyoung-Won Park · Ian
Barnett · Ian Buchan ·
Ian McMillan · Ian
Mond · Ian Randall · Ifer
Moore · Ilana Doran ·
Ines Fernandes · Ingrid
Olsen · Irene Mansfield ·
Irina Tzanova · Isabella
Livorni · Isabella
Weibrecht · Isobel
Dixon · J Collins ·
Jacinta Perez Gavilan
Torres · Jack Brown ·
Jack Fisher · Jacqueline
Haskell · Jacqueline
Lademann · Jacqueline
Ting Lin · Jacqueline
Vint · Jadie Lee · Jake
Nicholls · James Attlee ·
James Beck · James
Crossley · James
Cubbon · James
Lehmann · James
Lesniak · James
Portlock · James
Purdon · James
Scudamore · James
Tierney · James Ward ·
Jamie Cox · Jamie
Mollart · Jamie Walsh ·
Jane Fairweather · Jane
Roberts · Jane Roberts ·
Jane Woollard · Janet
Gilmore · Janette Ryan ·
Janne Støen · Jasmine
Gideon · Jayne Watson ·
JC Blake · Jeannie
Stirrup · Jeff Collins ·
Jeffrey Davies · Jenifer
Logie · Jennifer Arnold ·
Jennifer Bernstein ·

Jennifer Calleja · Jennifer Harvey · Jennifer Humbert · Jennifer M Lee · Jenny Booth · Jenny Huth · Jenny Newton · Jeremy Koenig · Jeremy Trombley · Jes Fernie · Jess Howard-Armitage · Jesse Berrett · Jesse Coleman · Jessica Kibler · Jessica Laine · Jessica Loveland · Jessica Martin · Jethro Soutar · Jim Boucherat · Jo Harding · Jo Lateu · Joanna Flower · Joanna Luloff · Joanne Marlow · Joao Pedro Bragatti Winckler · JoDee Brandon · Jodie Adams · Jodie Martire · Joelle Young · Johanna Eliasson · Johannes Menzel · Johannes Georg Zipp · John Berube · John Bogg · John Conway · John Coyne · John Down · John Gent · John Hodgson · John Kelly · John Royley · John Shaw · John Steigerwald · John Winkelman · John Wyatt · Jon Riches · Jon Talbot · Jonathan Blaney · Jonathan Huston · Jonathan Kiehlmann · Jonathan Ruppin · Jonathan Watkiss · Jorge Cino · Jorid Martinsen · Joseph Cooney · Joseph Hiller · Joseph Schreiber · Joshua Davis · Joy Paul · Jude Shapiro · Julia Peters · Julia Rochester · Julia Sutton-Mattocks · Julia Ellis Burnet · Julie Greenwalt · Juliet Swann · Justine Sless · K Elkes · Kaarina Hollo · Kapka Kassabova · Karen Faarbaek de Andrade Lima · Karen Waloschek · Kasim Husain · Kasper Haakansson · Kasper Hartmann · Kate Attwooll · Kate Gardner · Kate McCaughley · Kate Morgan · Katharina Liehr · Katharine Freeman · Katharine Robbins · Katherine El-Salahi · Katherine Gray · Katherine Mackinnon · Katherine Skala · Katherine Sotejeff-Wilson · Kathryn Cave · Kathryn Edwards · Kathryn Williams · Katie Brown · Katie Lewin · Katrina Thomas · Keith Fenton · Keith Walker · Kenneth Blythe · Kenneth Michaels · Kent McKernan · Kevin Maxwell · Khairunnisa Ibrahim · Kieron James · Kim Armstrong · Kim Smith · Kirsten Hey · Kirsty Doole · KL Ee · Klara Rešetič · Kris Ann Trimis · Kristin Djuve · Kristina Rudinskas · Krystine Phelps · Kylé Pienaar · Lana Selby · Lander Hawes · Lara Vergnaud · Larraine Gooch · Laura Batatota · Laura Brown · Laura Lea · Laurence Laluyaux · Laurie Sheck & Jim Peck · Lee Harbour · Leeanne Parker · Leigh Aitken · Leon Frey & Natalie Winwood · Leonie Schwab · Leonie Smith · Lesley Lawn · Lesley Naylor · Leslie Wines · Liam Elward · Liliana Lobato · Lindsay Brammer · Lindsey Stuart · Lindy van Rooyen · Line Langebek Knudsen · Linette Arthurton Bruno · Lisa Dillman · Liz Clifford · Liz Ketch · Liz Wilding · Lola Boorman · Lorna Bleach · Lottie Smith · Louise Foster · Louise Smith · Luc Verstraete · Lucia Rotheray · Lucia Whitney · Lucy Goy · Lucy Hariades · Lucy Moffatt · Luke Healey · Luke Williamson · Lula Belle · Lynn Martin · Lynne Bryan · Lysann Church · M Manfre · Mads Pihl Rasmussen · Maeve Lambe · Maggie Humm · Maggie Livesey · Maggie Redway · Mahan L Ellison & K Ashley Dickson · Malgorzata Rokicka · Margaret Briggs · Margaret Jull Costa · Maria Ahnhem Farrar · Marie Bagley · Marie Cloutier · Marie Donnelly · Marike Dokter · Marina Castledine · Marina Jones · Mario Cianci · Mario Sifuentez · Mark Dawson · Mark Sargent · Mark Sztyber · Mark Waters · Mark Whitelaw · Marlene Adkins · Martha Nicholson · Martha Stevns · Martin Brown · Martin Price · Martin Vosyka · Martin Whelton · Mary Carozza · Mary Heiss · Mary Nash · Mary Wang · Mary Ellen Nagle · Marzia Rahman · Mathieu Trudeau · Matt Davies · Matt Greene · Matt O'Connor · Matthew Adamson · Matthew Armstrong · Matthew Banash · Matthew Black · Matthew Francis · Matthew Geden · Matthew Gill · Matthew Hiscock · Matthew

Lowe · Matthew
Thomas · Matthew
Warshauer · Matthew
Woodman · Matty Ross ·
Maureen Karman ·
Maureen Pritchard ·
Max Cairnduff · Max
Garrone · Max
Longman · Meaghan
Delahunt · Megan
Muneeb · Megan
Wittling · Melissa
Apfelbaum · Melissa
Apfelbaum · Melissa
Beck · Melissa
Quignon-Finch ·
Melynda Nuss ·
Meredith Jones · Meryl
Wingfield · Michael
Aguilar · Michael
Bichko · Michael Gavin ·
Michael Kuhn · Michael
Mc Caughley · Michael
Moran · Michael
Schneiderman · Michael
Ward · Michael James
Eastwood · Michelle
Falkoff · Michelle
Lotherington · Michelle
Roberts · Mike Bittner ·
Mike Turner · Milla
Rautio · Milo
Waterfield · Miranda
Gold · Miriam McBride ·
Moray Teale · Morgan
Bruce · Morgan Lyons ·
MP Boardman · Myles
Nolan · N Tsolak ·
Namita Chakrabarty ·
Nan Craig · Nancy
Cooley · Nancy Oakes ·
Naomi Kruger · Natalie
Steer · Nathalie
Atkinson · Nathan
Dorr · Ned Vaught ·
Neferti Tadiar · Neil
George · Nicholas
Brown · Nick Chapman ·
Nick Flegel · Nick
James · Nick Nelson &
Rachel Eley · Nick
Rombes · Nick Sidwell ·
Nick Twemlow · Nicola
Hart · Nicola Mira ·
Nicola Sandiford ·
Nicole Matteini · Nikos

Lykouras · Nina
Alexandersen · Nina de
la Mer · Nina Moore ·
Nina Parish · Nina
Power · Olga
Brawanska · Olga
Zilberbourg · Olivia
Payne · Olivia Tweed ·
Pamela Ritchie · Pat
Bevins · Patricia
Appleyard · Patricia
Webbs · Patrick
McGuinness · Paul
Cray · Paul Daw · Paul
Jones · Paul Munday ·
Paul Myatt · Paul Scott ·
Paul Segal · Paula
Edwards · Paula Ely ·
Pavlos Stavropoulos ·
Penelope Hewett
Brown · Penny
Simpson · Pete
Stephens · Peter
McBain · Peter
McCambridge · Peter
Rowland · Peter Vilbig ·
Peter Vos · Peter Wells ·
Philip Carter · Philip
Lewis · Philip Lom ·
Philip Nulty · Philip
Scott · Philip Warren ·
Philipp Jarke · Pia
Ghosh-Roy · Piet Van
Bockstal · Pippa Tolfts ·
PM Goodman · Portia
Msimang · PRAH
Foundation · Puck
Askew · Rachael
Williams · Rachel
Andrews · Rachel
Carter · Rachel
Darnley-Smith · Rachel
Lasserson · Rachel Van
Riel · Rachel Wadham ·
Rachel Watkins · Ralph
Cowling · Ramon
Bloomberg · Rea Cris ·
Rebecca Braun · Rebecca
Carter · Rebecca Moss ·
Rebecca Rosenthal ·
Rhiannon Armstrong ·
Richard Ashcroft ·
Richard Bauer · Richard
Clifford · Richard Dew ·
Richard Gwyn · Richard
Mansell · Richard

Priest · Richard Shea ·
Richard Soundy ·
Richard Thomson ·
Rishi Dastidar · Robert
Gillett · Robert
Hamilton · Robert
Hannah · Robert
Hugh-Jones · Robin
Taylor · Roger Newton ·
Roger Ramsden · Roger
Salloch · Rory Dunlop ·
Rory Williamson ·
Rosalind May · Rosalind
Ramsay · Rosanna
Foster · Rose Crichton ·
Rosemary Gilligan ·
Rosie Pinhorn · Ross
Scott & Jimmy Gilmore ·
Ross Trenzinger ·
Rowan Sullivan ·
Roxanne O'Del Ablett ·
Royston Tester · Roz
Simpson · Rune
Salvesen · Rupert
Ziziros · Ruth Chitty ·
Ryan Grossman · Sabine
Griffiths · Sabrina
Uswak · Sally Baker ·
Sally Foreman · Sam
Gordon · Sam Reese ·
Sam Stern · Samantha
Murphy · Sara
Goldsmith · Sara
Sherwood · Sarah
Arboleda · Sarah
Forster · Sarah Jacobs ·
Sarah Lucas · Sarah
Moss · Sarah Pybus ·
Sarah Smith · Sarah
Watkins · Satara Lazar ·
Scott Chiddister · Sean
Birnie · Sean Kelly ·
Sean McGivern · Sejal
Shah · Seonad
Plowman · Sez Kiss · SH
Makdisi · Shannon
Knapp · Shaun
Whiteside · Shauna
Gilligan · Sheridan
Marshall · Sherman
Alexie · Shira Lob ·
Simon Armstrong ·
Simon Clark · Simon
Harley · Simon Pitney ·
Simon Robertson · Siriol
Hugh-Jones · SK Grout ·

Sonia McLintock · Sophia Wickham · Soren Murhart · ST Dabbagh · Stacy Rodgers · Stefano Mula · Stella Francis · Stephan Eggum · Stephanie Lacava · Stephanie Smee · Stephen Eisenhammer · Stephen Pearsall · Steven & Gitte Evans · Stu Sherman · Stuart Wilkinson · Susan Higson · Susan Irvine · Susie Roberson · Suzanne Lee · Sylvie Zannier-Betts · Tamara Larsen · Tamsin Dewé · Tania Hershman · Tara Roman · Teresa Griffiths · Teresa Werner · Terry Kurgan · The Mighty Douche Softball Team · Therese Oulton · Thomas Baker · Thomas Bell · Thomas Chadwick · Thomas Fritz · Thomas Mitchell · Thomas van den Bout · Tiffany Lehr · Tiffany Stewart · Tim Hopkins · Tim Jones · Tim Retzloff · Tim Scott · Tim Theroux · Timothy Nixon · Tina Andrews · Tina Rotherham-Winqvist · Toby Day · Toby Halsey · Toby Ryan · Tom Atkins · Tom Darby · Tom Franklin · Tom Gray · Tom Stafford · Tom Whatmore · Tony Bastow · Tony Messenger · Torna Russell-Hills · Tory Jeffay · Tracey Martin · Tracy Heuring · Tracy Northup · Treasa De Loughry · Trevor Wald · Val Challen · Valerie Sirr · Vanessa Dodd · Vanessa Nolan · Veronica Barnsley · Veronica Baruffati · Vicki White · Victor Meadowcroft · Victoria Adams · Victoria Huggins · Victoria Maitland · Vijay Pattisapu · Vikki O'Neill · Volker Welter · Walter Fircowycz · Walter Smedley · Wendy Langridge · Wendy Olson · William Dennehy · William Mackenzie · William Schwartz · Zachary Hope · Zack Frehlick · Zoë Brasier

OLIVIA ROSENTHAL is a French novelist and teacher of creative writing. She lectures at Université Paris VIII, where she and a colleague founded one of the first Creative Writing MA programmes in France. Rosenthal's work has won numerous prizes, including the Prix Wepler, the Prix du Livre Inter and the Prix Alexandre-Vialatte.

SOPHIE LEWIS translates from French and Portuguese. She has translated Stendhal, Verne, Marcel Aymé, Violette Leduc, Emmanuelle Pagano, Jean-Luc Raharimanana, Sheyla Smanioto and João Gilberto Noll, among others.